"Sasha…"

She flattened her palms against her ears, trying to shut out the ghostly voice.

"Go away," Sasha whispered back. "Please, Nadine, leave me alone…." A shudder wracked her body. Had she lost her mind? She was arguing with a ghost. But was Nadine a ghost? Was she really dead? No one had found her body, just the blood.

Suddenly Sasha heard another cry. Annie's. The storm must have awakened the child.

"Sasha…"

She ignored the whisper as she kicked back the covers. The nanny was closer, but Sasha had to go to the little girl. She needed Annie, needed to hold her to soothe herself. Her bare feet padded against the worn runner as she felt her way down the hall. The nursery door stood open and lightning flashed through the window, illuminating the room where the child slept peacefully again in the crib.

In the corner, the rocker moved to and fro….

Dear Harlequin Intrigue Reader,

Spring is in the air and we have a month of fabulous books for you to curl up with as the March winds howl outside:

- Familiar is back on the prowl, in Caroline Burnes's *Familiar Texas*. And *Rocky Mountain Maneuvers* marks the conclusion of Cassie Miles's COLORADO CRIME CONSULTANTS trilogy.

- Jessica Andersen brings us an exciting medical thriller, *Covert M.D.*

- Don't miss the next ECLIPSE title, Lisa Childs's *The Substitute Sister*.

- Definitely check out our April lineup. Debra Webb is starting THE ENFORCERS, an exciting new miniseries you won't want to miss. Also look for a special 3-in-1 story from Rebecca York, Ann Voss Peterson and Patricia Rosemoor called *Desert Sons*.

Each month, Harlequin Intrigue brings you a variety of heart-stopping romantic suspense and chilling mystery. Don't miss a single book!

Sincerely,

Denise O'Sullivan
Senior Editor
Harlequin Intrigue

THE SUBSTITUTE SISTER
LISA CHILDS

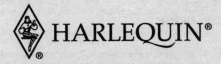

TORONTO • NEW YORK • LONDON
AMSTERDAM • PARIS • SYDNEY • HAMBURG
STOCKHOLM • ATHENS • TOKYO • MILAN • MADRID
PRAGUE • WARSAW • BUDAPEST • AUCKLAND

To Stacy Boyd—my helpful, insightful editor.

To Kimberly Duffy w/a Lindsey Brookes—
for unwavering friendship and support—love you!

ISBN 0-373-22834-1

THE SUBSTITUTE SISTER

Copyright © 2005 by Lisa Childs-Theeuwes

www.eHarlequin.com

Printed in U.S.A.

ABOUT THE AUTHOR

Lisa Childs has been writing since she could first form sentences. At eleven she won her first writing award and was interviewed by the local newspaper. That story's plot revolved around a kidnapping, probably something she wished on any of her six siblings. A Halloween birthday predestined a life of writing intrigue. She enjoys the mix of suspense and romance.

Readers can write to Lisa at P.O. Box 139, Marne, MI 49435 or visit her at her Web site www.lisachilds.com.

Books by Lisa Childs

HARLEQUIN INTRIGUE
664—RETURN OF THE LAWMAN
720—SARAH'S SECRETS
758—BRIDAL RECONNAISSANCE
834—THE SUBSTITUTE SISTER

CAST OF CHARACTERS

Sasha Michaelson—She's lost her twin on Sunset Island, but she's in danger of losing her heart and her life, too.

Reed Blakeslee—The lawman's determined to protect Sasha, no matter the risk...physically or emotionally.

Nadine Michaelson—She's always resented her twin—enough to lure her to danger?

Charles Norder—Sasha's ex-fiancé had left her for her sister. How obsessed had he remained?

Albert Jorgen—The lawyer handled all of Nadine's personal affairs.

Roger Scott—How resentful was he that Nadine had stolen his inheritance?

Mrs. Arnold—The housekeeper served herself first.

Jerry—Does the gardener know where all the secrets are buried?

Barbie—The young nanny resents her new employer as much as her missing one.

Annie—The toddler now calls her aunt Mommy, but will she lose this one, too?

The Scott Mansion—The old Victorian house is alive with hatred and ghosts.

Chapter One

Sasha stepped before the long oval mirror, peering at her reflection to adjust her veil. The gauzy lace hindered her sight that day, her wedding day; foolish trust blinded her every other day. Frustration jangled her nerves, so that when she lifted the veil, her shaking fingers rent the fabric, leaving it in tatters across her face.

But it wasn't her face staring back at her through the suddenly fogging glass. It was her twin standing there, shiny black hair flowing around the shoulders of the lacy white gown, the tattered veil mingling with her thick lashes and bright-blue eyes. It was Nadine's laughter that rang out, shattering the silence of the night and pulling Sasha from her dream.

Instead of the bright sunshine of the back room of the chapel in her dream, Sasha opened her eyes to thick darkness. But the enveloping night didn't slow her racing heart or soothe her raw nerves. She hadn't had that dream in years. Had the stress of her crazy day working at the high school inspired it? Counseling teens had always stressed her out. Why have the dream now?

And why did her twin's laughter still ring in her ears?

No, not Nadine's laughter. The phone. With shaking hands, Sasha fumbled for the receiver, knocked it onto the floor, then used the cord to reel it up to her ear. "Hello…" she stammered.

"Ms. Michaelson?" a man asked. The deep rumble of his voice rasped along her oversensitive nerve endings.

"Yes?" She wasn't sure of her identity herself. Not after that dream.

She squinted at the illuminated face of the alarm clock on the bedside table. After midnight? Nobody called her after midnight. Her heart rate accelerated, and her hand trembled on the phone. "Who is this?"

"Sheriff Blakeslee."

A sheriff? Sasha wrestled with the covers to sit up against the hard oak headboard, trying to clear the sleep and the awful dream from her mind. Had something happened to her parents? Had one of the kids she counseled gotten into trouble?

"What? Why…" she sputtered.

"Maybe I should have sent an officer over, but I felt I needed to tell you myself."

"Tell me what?" Her heart hammered so hard now, she pressed a fist against it. Something bad had happened. A sheriff wouldn't call after midnight for any other reason.

"About your sister, Ms. Michaelson." The man's voice vibrated with emotion. Sadness? Regret?

Sasha had her share of those feelings when it came to Nadine. She shivered, drawing the flannel comforter back around the shoulders of the faded football jersey she wore as a nightgown. Even in spring, the nights were cold in Michigan. The dream and the call had her shivering despite the warmth of the blankets.

"This is about Nadine?" She was the only sister Sasha had. Her twin. "What's happened?"

What had Nadine done? What kind of trouble was she in this time? Sasha hadn't heard from or about her twin in years, hadn't even thought about her much… until tonight…until that dream….

"Ms. Michaelson, there's…well, we believe your sister's dead. I'm very sorry for your loss."

Her loss? She'd lost her sister ten years ago when as a high school senior, Nadine had run away from home. "Uh, umm…" Shock numbed her brain, slowing her thought processes. "Nadine's dead?"

No, she couldn't accept that. It wasn't possible. Nadine's laughter still hung in the night.

"You're wrong," she told the sheriff, angry with him, with Nadine, with herself for all the lost years between them. "It can't be her."

"I waited until the DNA evidence confirmed—"

"No!" God, no, not Nadine. She was too young, much too young to die.

"I know this is devastating, and you're probably concerned about Annie. But she's all right. She hasn't been harmed."

"Annie?" Who was he talking about?

The deep voice roughened. "Annie is Nadine's daughter, your niece."

"My niece?" God, she hadn't known. She and Nadine hadn't talked in five years. Her eyes burned as tears swam to the surface, blurring the shadows of her dark bedroom. They would never be able to talk again, never have a chance to form the sisterly relationship they should have had as twins.

The sheriff's voice rumbled in her ear again, "Your sister has—had—a two-year-old daughter."

Sasha's breath caught in her lungs, pressing against her heart. A two-year-old? A baby, really. And she'd lost her mother. "She's all right?"

"Yes, she is," he said, relief apparent in his soft sigh. Then he asked, "You didn't know about Annie?"

Maybe it was the anonymity of a voice in the darkness, like a priest in a dimly lit confessional, that brought out her admission to a stranger. "I don't know anything about my sister. I don't even know where she's been living, where you're calling from." The last place she'd seen Nadine had been in her dream. "We haven't talked in years."

Five years after Nadine had first run away from home, Sasha had tracked down her sister to make sure she would come to her wedding. A wedding that hadn't taken place *because* Sasha had found Nadine.

"Yet in the event of anything happening to her, she named *you* as guardian of her daughter." The sheriff's voice held a trace of bitterness.

"Wh-what about the child's father?" Was Sasha's

former fiancé Annie's daddy? No, she doubted he and Nadine had lasted that long. Her sister had only taken him away to hurt and humiliate Sasha. Nadine had used him like she'd once bragged that she'd often used men.

Had the sheriff been involved with Nadine? From the emotion roughening his voice, she suspected he had.

"Your sister was a single mother."

"But the little girl's father…" Would have more right to the child than she would. Not that Sasha didn't want Annie, this child she hadn't known existed. Nadine's child.

"Annie's birth certificate says father unknown."

So many questions burned in Sasha's mind, the most important being, why had Nadine named *her* guardian of her daughter? Nadine had always resented her. Despite being twins, they'd shared nothing but the same face.

"Sheriff, I need to know—"

"You need to come to Sunset Island," the sheriff prompted, "for Annie."

The child was most important; the questions could wait.

"I'll tell you everything I know when you get here," the sheriff added.

Even if he had been involved with Nadine, how much would he know about her life? Nadine had never been the type to share, not even with her twin.

How had she died? The sheriff might know that, but would he know the rest? Would he know any of the reasons why Nadine had done the things she'd done? Why she'd run away from her family in the first place?

Now she was lost to them forever.

Poor Nadine.

Poor Annie.

Sasha flipped on the light by the bed and frantically hunted down a piece of paper and a pen as she blinked back her tears. She didn't have time for them now; she needed to be strong for her motherless niece. "How do I get to Sunset Island? Where is it?"

"In Lake Michigan. You can take a flight into Escanaba. I'll have a deputy meet you at the airport and drive you to the ferry that'll bring you to the island."

"I'll take the first flight there." Although Sasha had always believed they lived in different worlds, her sister had stayed in the same state, barely, on an island. She couldn't imagine Nadine living anywhere but a bustling, exciting city. Now she wasn't living at all.

"You're sure…Nadine's really dead?"

He said just one last thing before hanging up. "Yes." The single word held a wealth of emotion, regret, guilt, sadness….

Her sister had meant something to the sheriff with the deep, rumbly voice. And as grief and guilt rushed in, lying heavy on her aching heart, Sasha realized that the angry words spoken between her sister and her, the grudge she'd harbored these past five years—none of it mattered now. Nothing mattered but that Nadine was really gone this time.

It didn't matter that the only vow Sasha had made on what should have been her wedding day was that she would never let Nadine hurt her again. That vow had been broken, along with Sasha's heart, with the loss of her twin.

And the last traces of Nadine's laughter died away in the darkness…leaving only the jarring sound of Sasha's sobs.

REED STARED AT THE PHONE he'd just put back on the charger. Her sister hadn't exactly broken down over Nadine's death. In fact she'd seemed more shocked to learn that she was an aunt.

He rubbed a hand over his jaw, over the stubble he hadn't had time to shave off. God, he wasn't being fair. Everybody handled loss in their own way. But she had admitted that she'd known nothing about Nadine's life. And Nadine had never mentioned her.

Then why give her Annie?

He strode across the small living room to the open door of the spare bedroom. Light spilled into the room, falling across the face of the child sleeping on the mattress he'd pulled onto the floor. He didn't have a crib, didn't even know if she'd still sleep in one at two years old. Because of his ex, he'd never learned the things he'd wanted to learn about kids. Never had any of his own.

But in his heart Annie was his. He'd brought her into the world. He had been the first to touch her soft, tear-damp cheek. The first person who had met her crystal-blue gaze. And Nadine, grateful for his help delivering her child when they'd been snowed in on the island, had asked him to be Annie's godfather.

So, why not her guardian?

He eased down onto the floor next to the mattress, the bare wood boards hard and cold beneath his worn-denim-covered legs. Even in spring the temperature still dropped below freezing at night on the island. Reaching across the mattress, he tugged a soft blanket up over the comforter. Then he tucked the baby-blue satin edge under her chin.

Annie's security blanket. The kid would need that blanket more than ever. How much security would she have now that her mother was dead and she would be turned over to a stranger?

His gut twisted, anger and regret churning inside him. He'd known something was going on with Nadine, but despite sharing the birth of her child, they hadn't shared much else. Nadine's secrets had died with her.

Violently.

During his years as a Detroit Homicide detective, he'd seen a lot of gruesome things. But the blood pooled on the marble floor and dripping from the walls of the foyer of Nadine's house had affected him strongly because it had spilled from a woman he'd known...personally. Maybe would have known more personally if the timing had been different.

Even now, more than two years later, bitterness over his divorce burned in him. And Nadine's heart had been heavy with the secrets she carried and refused to share. But because of his role as Annie's godfather, they'd been friends.

And now she was gone.

Where the hell had the sick bastard hidden her body? Reed hadn't found it yet. So Nadine's survivors would have nothing to bury but memories.

He brushed the tangle of black curls back from the little girl's face, then stroked his finger over her soft cheek. A shaky little breath sighed out of her rosebud lips. Would Annie even remember her mother? She was so young.

If her aunt took her away, would the child remember him?

Perhaps the woman would stay on Sunset Island? Not damned likely. Not even with the inheritance of the old Scott mansion would a young woman willingly endure the isolation of a mostly undeveloped island where motor vehicles weren't even allowed.

So why had Nadine? After she'd inherited the mansion from her former employer, why hadn't she sold it and left for the brighter attractions of a city? What had she been hiding, or from whom?

And why in the hell hadn't he pushed harder to find out?

If he had, she might be alive. But he'd been afraid, for Annie's sake, of what he might find. Even though he'd found no evidence to support some of the rumors whispered around the small, gossipy community about Nadine, he could have dug deeper into her past. But then he might have found something to take her away from Annie. Now someone else had.

And now that it was too late to save her, he'd started the deep digging in the hopes of uncovering the identity of her killer. That was one of the reasons he'd given up Homicide and moved to a small rural department where the most violent thing that had ever happened was a bar fight. He'd gotten sick of being called when it was too late, when he couldn't save the victim any-more…like he should have saved Nadine.

He lifted his gaze toward the window, not that he could see anything outside the dark glass. Fog and the blackness of a starless night wrapped around the small cottage. As soon as the sun had dropped from the sky, thick moisture had risen from the cold surface of the lake and drifted across the island, seeming to isolate it from the mainland even more than the miles of water surrounding it.

No, Sasha Michaelson wouldn't be staying.

His ex-wife hadn't even liked to visit when he'd bought the cottage on the island years ago, although like many other things, she hadn't admitted her displeasure until their divorce. She would never have given up the bustle of Detroit for the backwardness of Sunset Island. She'd pointed out that few women would, that he'd never have the family he wanted if he moved there.

Fudge shops were the main retail store. For any other shopping or entertainment, an islander had to take a ferry to the Upper Peninsula and from there another hour's drive to a city. The isolation was so extreme few people stayed year-round, but Nadine had. He had de-livered Annie because Nadine had been determined to have her child on the island…and there had been no one else around.

Before Nadine's murder, he'd considered the isolation of the island the perfect atmosphere to raise children, safe from all the dangers of the world. He'd seen those dangers up close and personal while he'd been a homicide detective. He hadn't ever thought that kind of danger would visit Sunset Island. But it had.

That was why, despite the nanny at the mansion, Reed hadn't taken Annie back there. He wanted to keep her close and safe…until he had to hand her over to a stranger.

THE CHOPPY WAVES jerked the ferry up and down. In addition to the rooster spray shooting out of the rear of the boat, a fine mist rose from the lake. Damp and cold, Sasha huddled inside her coat, shivering. Maybe she should have gone below, as the deputy suggested, but she'd been drawn to the deck, to the anger of the water and the closeness of the low-hanging dark clouds that suited her mood.

She hadn't slept since the sheriff's call despite the wait she'd had before the first flight available between Grand Rapids and Escanaba. Packing had only taken her a short while. The rest of the time she'd spent looking through the family albums her parents had entrusted to her while they RV'd across America in their retirement.

Old-fashioned and on a fixed income, they'd refused to get a cell phone, so she had no way of contacting them to let them know about their other daughter.

That she was dead.

They would call her on Sunday night, as always. She'd left a message on her machine for them to call her cell. And then she'd have to break the news as the sheriff had broken it to her…over the phone.

How was she going to tell them? "Nadine's dead." That simply? But nothing was simple about this. She didn't even know how her sister had died. Their parents would want to know that.

Nadine was their biggest regret. Instead of supporting her through her difficulties, they'd threatened and punished her. The bad grades hadn't been Nadine's fault; she'd been dyslexic. But their parents hadn't understood that. If she'd tried harder, they'd argued, she could have gotten grades as good as Sasha's. After all, they were twins.

But so very, very different. Never more so than now that one of them lived and one had died.

Maybe Nadine had been right all along. Everything bad always happened to her. But was it, as their parents claimed, because of the choices she'd made?

Somehow, despite their long separation, Sasha was sure if given the choice, Nadine would have chosen life. If not for herself…then for her daughter. Wouldn't she? Wouldn't the responsibility of a child have caused her wild sister to settle down?

Nadine had a daughter.

That was the other thing she had to tell her parents. "I'm an aunt. You're grandparents."

Nadine's running away had aged them. Could they handle these shocks?

God, she hoped so…because she needed someone to talk to. The sheriff's deputy had barely said two words to her since picking her up at the airport. His first reaction had been an audible gasp, then she had explained that she was—had been—Nadine's twin.

A dark shadow fell across the deck, and Sasha lifted her gaze toward the sky. The thick clouds had shifted even lower, an impenetrable layer blocking out the sun. A sense of foreboding chilled her soul, and she shivered. She was being silly, letting the deputy's reaction affect her. She wasn't her sister's ghost, she was her niece's guardian.

From his end of the bench seat on the ferry, the deputy kept shooting her furtive glances. When she caught him, red flooded his pitted cheeks. He reminded her of the teenagers she counseled at the high school; heck, he probably wasn't much older.

Today, Sasha felt a lot older. It had nothing to do with sleep loss and everything to do with Nadine's loss. Despite that vow she'd made, she'd always had a little hope in her heart that they'd be able to make amends someday. That they'd be able to form that almost sacred relationship that twins were supposed to have.

Now Sasha felt no hope. Although she was used to counseling teens, she knew nothing about babies. At two, wasn't Annie still a baby? Could she talk? Did she know her mother was dead?

Was she devastated? As devastated as Sasha?

Fear gripped Sasha, clenching her already knotted stomach muscles. As her sister, as her *twin,* she'd failed

Nadine. She should have been there for her, should have stopped her from running away all those years ago. Would she fail Nadine's daughter, too?

Tired of the thoughts running through her head, she turned toward the deputy. "Can you tell me how my sister died?"

The sheriff hadn't given her any details, hadn't given her much of anything but a sense of disapproval. Not all siblings were close. She shouldn't feel guilty for knowing nothing about Nadine's life, but she did. The guilt gnawed at her, leaving her feeling hollow inside.

The deputy's Adam's apple bobbed as he swallowed hard then shook his head. "No, Miss Michaelson."

"You don't know?" Or he didn't want to tell her? Maybe it had been suicide? No, Nadine wouldn't have done that. She'd always been so independent, so strong. But if it had been an accident, surely the sheriff would have said.

"Sheriff Blakeslee said he'd tell you everything when we meet him on the island, ma'am." And from his diffident tone, the young deputy was too in awe of the sheriff to ever consider disobeying a command from the man.

She could make him talk; that was her job. If she could make teenagers open up, she could get the deputy to spill. But she had to admit that she didn't want to hear the particulars from him. She wanted his boss to tell her. Sheriff Blakeslee was only a voice in the darkness to her, but she felt closer to him than this young man. She'd already shared something with him, the horrible news of her sister's death.

"How long before we reach the island?" Maybe it was the violent waves that made her think miles of water had passed under the ferry's jumping hull.

"Not much longer. It's a two-hour ride total."

She didn't know much about boats even though she'd been raised in the Great Lakes state. How many miles did a boat travel in two hours? How many miles from civilization was the island? And why had Nadine chosen to live there? "Does the sheriff live there, too?"

"He divides his time between Whiskey Bay and the island. He bought a place on Sunset years ago when he was still a detective in Detroit." The wind ruffled the young man's fine hair as he shook his head, probably unable to understand why someone would have moved from Detroit to the remoteness of the north country.

"Did he retire here?" Although she'd only heard his voice, she doubted he was old enough to be drawing a pension.

The deputy shook his head again. "No, he's only in his thirties, the youngest sheriff we've ever had. But with all his years on the force in Detroit, he's got more law enforcement experience than any sheriff before him."

Did he need it? Would he use it on Sunset Island? She peered up at the dark clouds and shivered.

She preferred talking about the sheriff, talking about anything, rather than tormenting herself with regrets over Nadine's death. She'd had so much living to do yet, had a child to raise.

And now Sasha had that responsibility. Unable to

fight the guilt any longer, she found herself asking, "Can you tell me about my sister?"

Like, who had fathered her baby and why wasn't he around to be guardian for his child?

The young man wouldn't meet her eyes, glancing out over the rolling waves instead. And in the distance, through the mist rising from the water, a dark shadow formed. The island. "Miss Michaelson, the sheriff can tell you everything. He was really close to your sister."

How close? Intimate. From the nervous shift of the deputy's gaze, she suspected as much.

Would the sheriff tell her everything? Or, out of loyalty to Nadine, would he resent her as much as her sister always had? Was it resentment that had kept Nadine from telling her about her niece? Or had it been because Sasha had told her she never wanted to talk to or see her again?

Sasha had never been so angry as she'd been the last time she'd seen Nadine, had never held a grudge the way she had these past five years. Now guilt and grief replaced the anger, threatening more tears. She blinked hard. She couldn't cry now, not in front of anyone. She'd suffered that humiliation when she'd been left at the altar five years ago; she wouldn't do it again.

And as for the sheriff, she'd get him to tell her everything about her sister. If she could handle surly teenagers, she could handle a resentful sheriff.

What had Nadine been to him? Lover? If he were half as attractive as he'd sounded on the phone, Nadine would have gone after him.

Sasha wanted to flat-out ask the deputy how involved his boss had been with her sister, but for her answer she'd only get a deeper blush out of him. So she would save that question for the sheriff along with all her others. And she wouldn't stop asking until she got her answers about Nadine's life and…death.

The ferry neared the island, where a large dock jutted out of a rocky shore. From that area, a hill rose up, dotted with houses. Small cottages were squeezed in between large, elaborate homes. Here, so far north, the leaves were little more than buds on the trees, and the early-spring gloom hung in low clouds over the island. A chill raced over her skin, the sense of foreboding returning with more force. She shouldn't have come here. But she'd had to…for Annie. And the chill—it was probably just the cold spring wind.

Late April. She'd had over a month left of the school year, but after the sheriff had called her, she'd called the principal and arranged for a leave.

"We're lucky the weather's been so warm," the deputy remarked with a sigh, probably with relief that he had found a safe subject and that the island…and the sheriff…were near.

"Warm?" she asked, as she huddled inside her winter jacket. Having visited the Upper Peninsula in the spring before, she'd known to wear heavier clothes. With the jacket she wore thick corduroy jeans and a sweater.

"Oh, yeah, we had major snowstorms this time last year. It's so nice this year. The sheriff, along with some other sheriffs in the surrounding areas, even had their golf outing already."

"Before or after my sister died?" she asked, frustration sharpening her tone. She wanted answers. The long ferry ride had given her mind time to formulate more questions, the first being why had Nadine chosen to live in such isolation?

The deputy's cheeks colored again. "It was actually the day your sister—look, we're here now."

The ferry pulled to the dock. Sasha's breath caught over the enormity of the situation. This was where Nadine had lived and where, Sasha assumed, she'd died. This was where Sasha would meet her niece for the first time, where she would pick up the child who was now her responsibility. This poor little motherless girl. Would she be terrified of her aunt, of this woman she'd never met but who looked eerily like her mother?

The deputy hovered at her side as she walked down the gangplank toward the dock. The wind whipped up, tangling her hair around her face. She nearly stumbled, then stopped and turned her attention to the waiting people. The small crowd shifted as she joined them, people staring, some gasping as the deputy had, a general sense of fear emanating from them. She ignored their reactions as best she could but was thankful for the deputy standing beside her as she looked for the sheriff.

"There he is." The deputy gestured toward a dark-haired man. He didn't wear a uniform, but he didn't need it.

His height separated him from everyone else, giving him an air of authority. He had to be well over six feet with shoulders so broad she was tempted to lay her weary head on one and weep the tears burning inside her for her sister's loss. The temptation surprised her, as did the quick flare of attraction she felt for him. For five years she hadn't allowed herself either weakness.

Then she saw the child in his arms, the little girl pressed close to his chest. She looked exactly the way Sasha and Nadine had looked as curly-haired toddlers.

Crystal-blue eyes widened as Annie stared at her, then a soft voice called out, "Mommy!"

Little arms reached for her, but Sasha froze, her reaction having nothing to do with the chill wind whipping around the open dock. Fear paralyzed her, holding her feet to the planks. She hadn't been able to save Nadine from the life she'd chosen, a life that had led to her death. How could she accept the responsibility of raising Nadine's child? What if she let them both down?

The sheriff walked toward her. His long, jeans-clad legs carrying him to her in a couple of strides. Despite the cold, he wore only a denim shirt with his faded jeans, the cuffs rolled to his elbows. His forearms, thick with muscle, cradled the little girl with no effort. His jaw, lightly stubbled with hair as dark as that brushing the collar of his shirt, was hard and clenched as he stared down at her. The gloom of the dark clouds shadowed his eyes, but the green gleamed vividly.

She shivered, not from the cold but from the awareness tingling across her skin. Last night his voice had rasped along her nerves, but today his stare was so intense, so intimate, it weakened her knees.

Despite the howl of the wind whipping up and the resumed conversation of the small, milling crowd, she caught the emotional rumble of his deep voice as he whispered, "Nadine?"

Chills chased away the nerves. Nadine? Although he stared at her, she wasn't the woman he very obviously wanted to see.

Nadine.

He must have loved her sister.

She had come to Sunset Island to collect Annie, to serve as her niece's substitute mother. And that was the only substitute she would ever serve for her sister. As much as she lacked confidence in her parenting abilities, she lacked even more in the bedroom. She knew she could never replace her sister there.

Chapter Two

He had known she was dead even before the crime-scene techs had verified that nobody could live with that much blood loss, which could have only been caused by the severing of a main artery. With DNA testing they had also verified that the blood was Nadine's.

The woman standing before him now didn't bear a single scratch that he could see, but he was tempted to pull back her collar to check. She was pale, her eyes the same vivid crystal blue of Annie's, the only color in her face. The wind tousled her long, black hair, swirling it in an ebony cloud around the shoulders of her blue jacket.

God, she was beautiful. He sucked in a quick breath of crisp air.

And she wasn't just a sister. She was Nadine's identical twin. "Sasha Michaelson."

She nodded. "Yes, and you're Sheriff Blakeslee? And this is Annie?"

The little girl reached for her, again calling out, "Mommy."

The woman didn't extend her arms to the child. Didn't she have any compassion? How could a woman this cold nurture a baby? "You look exactly like your sister." Beautiful and unapproachable. "She's confused."

"Annie, I'm your aunt. Your Aunt Sasha," she said to the child, her voice soft as she tried to explain.

Annie snuggled her head into his shoulder again; she must have recognized the difference. Despite identical faces, they didn't sound alike. Sasha's voice wasn't as husky as her sister's.

Reed patted the little girl's back, trying to soothe her the way he would a distraught crime victim, which in a way Annie was. Her mother's murder had affected her, too. It didn't matter how much this woman looked like Nadine, to Annie she was still a stranger. How could he turn the child over to her? "Ms. Michaelson—"

"Did I—should I have let her think…" Her voice cracked, and she shivered.

"Come on, let's get out of the wind," he said, leading her away from the dock. When his deputy moved to follow, he turned back toward him. "Tommy, I've got it from here. You can take the ferry back to Whiskey Bay. I need you to help Bruce at the office."

"But, Sheriff Blakeslee…"

The kid wanted to be where the excitement was. The biggest thing to have ever happened in the far-reaching area that was Reed's jurisdiction was Nadine's murder. But it was so much more to Reed, so much more personal. Maybe he'd thought he'd been acting as her friend by not digging into her past, but she might be alive if he had. And now, because she was dead, he had to dig. "I need you there."

"Yes…yes, sir," the young man stammered. While he didn't immediately head back to the ferry, he didn't follow when Reed started walking again.

Sasha Michaelson glanced back toward the deputy, probably wishing she could take the next ferry away from Sunset Island, too. "There are no cars?"

"Nope. We could take a horse-drawn carriage, but my house isn't far from here."

"House?"

"I don't have an office on the island. Nothing's ever really happened here." Until now. "A drunken brawl or two at one of the bars. And then I take them to the jail and office on the mainland."

"By ferry?"

"There's a sheriff's boat." He could have sent it for her, but he'd wanted it close…in case of emergency.

From the dock a cobblestone lane headed into the little town where the shops, restaurants and inns were. Reed led her the opposite direction, down a gravel path toward the houses. His cottage wasn't much closer than the Scott Mansion, but he wasn't ready to take her, or Annie, to the big house where Nadine had been savagely murdered, where her blood still stained the foyer.

Annie hadn't been home when her mother was killed. The nanny had taken her for a walk, so she hadn't seen anything. For that, but not much else, Reed could be grateful.

The problem was no one else had seen anything, either. No witnesses and no body made Nadine's murder tough to solve. But he would. He owed both Nadine and her daughter justice. He would find the killer, whether he'd left the island or still lived among them.

He touched Sasha Michaelson's back, turning her down the path toward his small, fieldstone cottage. She wasn't very tall, her head barely as high as his shoulder. And despite the bulky jacket and heavy pants, he could tell her frame was delicate. Like Nadine's.

He'd felt protective of Nadine and Annie. And it tore him apart that he hadn't been able to protect Nadine from death or Annie from the loss of her mother.

But he didn't feel protective of Sasha Michaelson. It was something else that flared inside him, something he hadn't felt in so long that he barely recognized it as the hot sting of desire.

"Nice," she murmured as she passed through the door he held open for her.

His ex-wife had hated the place for being too cramped, too primitive. A fire still burned in the grate, casting a warm glow over the hardwood floor. Sasha walked toward it, her hands out. "I forgot gloves," she said. "I thought I'd thought of everything, but I forgot gloves."

Reed caught the rising note of hysteria in her voice. Maybe she wasn't cold and unemotional. Maybe she was just scared. He glanced down at Annie's face. The child had fallen asleep in his arms, not a surprise after her restless night. He shouldered open the door to the spare bedroom and laid her on the mattress on the floor. Because of the chill in the room, he didn't bother removing her coat and just pulled the comforter over her legs.

When he rose to his feet, he found Sasha in the doorway, watching him and her niece. "She's so little," she said in a hushed whisper. "Just a baby, isn't she?"

"She'd argue that if she was awake," he said with a short chuckle. The little girl knew many words other than Mommy, had even gotten good at stringing some into basic sentences. She was at the age of wonder and development, and her mother would miss it all. If only Nadine had trusted him enough to tell him what had been troubling her…

"She talks?"

"She's very smart," he said, not bothering to disguise his pride in the child.

Sasha must have caught it because her eyes narrowed. Then she shivered again. He brushed past her, resisting the urge to slide an arm around her, as he walked back into the living room, his boots clunking against the floor. He didn't worry about Annie waking, Nadine had always said she was a sound sleeper. He worried about his reaction to Annie's aunt, about his urge to touch her.

Sasha stood in the doorway another minute, staring at her sleeping niece before she turned to him. "Does she know her mother's dead?"

He shook his head. "I don't think so."

"You haven't told her?"

"It's not my place." Nadine had had a legal document drawn up stating that fact, but in Reed's heart, he knew it was very much his place...as Annie's was with him.

"I have to tell her?"

"That's up to you, Miss Michaelson." And he did try to curb his bitterness. She didn't deserve it.

She lifted her hands, then let them drop back to her sides. "I don't know what to do...."

"You're in shock." He saw that now, as well as the fear that widened her crystal-blue eyes. More guilt plagued him for his lack of sensitivity.

Pride lifted her chin as she made a visible effort to pull herself together. "I'm just worried about her, about Annie. Losing her mother..."

"Yeah." He couldn't say any more, emotion choked his voice. A small kitchen was hidden behind the fireplace. He ducked around to splash coffee into two mugs. "Here, this'll warm up your hands."

And maybe Annie would warm her heart. She kept glancing toward the bedroom, alert to any murmur the child uttered in her sleep. She accepted the mug, barely distracted from her vigilance over her niece.

Still looking toward the bedroom, she asked, "How did my sister die?"

He didn't want to tell her, didn't want to reveal the gory details. "In her home," he said instead. Nadine should have been safe there, should have been safe on

Sunset Island. But since her murder, Reed couldn't see the island as a sanctuary. Until Nadine's killer was caught, an aura of danger would engulf the island like the fog that wrapped around it every night.

She glanced toward him, irritation flashing in her blue eyes. "I didn't ask where. I asked how."

She was good at pulling herself together, her voice strong now. Maybe she could handle the truth. And even if she couldn't, she had a right to know some of it. "She was murdered."

She didn't even flinch.

"You're not surprised."

"If it had been an accident, you would have said on the phone. You didn't. I expected the worst."

"Sounds like everyone always expected the worst of Nadine." Himself included. The things he'd found in her past, while some criminal, hadn't been as bad as he'd thought, nothing that should have cost her Annie or her life.

Sasha flinched, then squeezed her eyes shut. "That's not fair."

"Hell, no," he said, anger eating at him. But he wasn't angry with her. "None of it's fair. It's not fair that Nadine won't be alive to watch her child grow up, and it's not fair that Annie's lost her mother."

A tear slipped from under Sasha's thick lashes and slid down her cheek. His gut clenched. God, he hated tears. He'd rather face an armed suspect than a weeping woman. His ex had learned that fast and used it against him. Hell, even Annie knew how to play the waterworks. Was that the reason for Sasha's silent tears? Manipulation?

To get what she wanted? But what did she want? Sympathy? Forgiveness? He doubted he was the person she wanted it from. No, that person was dead and had died with whatever had kept the sisters from speaking for so many years still between them. He could see the guilt in her eyes, in her refusal to meet his gaze. He recognized guilt because he carried his own share of it, over his failure to protect Nadine from whatever or whomever she'd feared.

Did Sasha carry the guilt for whatever had caused their rift? Or was it guilt that she had carried a grudge over whatever her sister had done to her? Either way, the burden was just as heavy on her thin shoulders.

He gripped his mug harder so he wouldn't reach for her, so he wouldn't pull her into his arms to offer comfort…or more. Desire gripped his gut, knotting the muscles. God, she was beautiful. And that wasn't fair, either…not to a man who'd been alone too damned long.

"Do you know who? Have you arrested anyone?" she asked, blinking back the rest of her tears.

Would she shed them later, when she was alone? Would they be as silent as those that had escaped down her face here, or would she let loose wrenching sobs? And would there be anyone to hold her while she cried?

She had come alone to the island and had answered the phone last night. She still bore her maiden name, but that didn't mean she didn't have a significant other, that she wouldn't provide Annie with the father he'd tried so hard to be.

"What?" he asked, shaking off his thoughts with a concentrated effort.

"Do you know who killed my sister?"

"Not yet." But he damn well would. He might not be able to raise Annie, but he could give her justice for her mother.

"Your deputy said something that made me think you weren't here when it happened."

"No, I wasn't. I'm not on the island that much. I divide my time between here, the town of Whiskey Bay and the surrounding areas. Sunset Island is only part of my jurisdiction." But he hadn't been at work that day, anywhere.

He'd been playing a damned game of golf with some of his law enforcement friends. "I was with a sheriff from Winter Falls, over by Traverse City, and some others." He might not ever forgive himself for not being on duty when Nadine had needed him, and from the disapproval tightening Sasha's lips, he figured she wouldn't, either.

"So I guess that gives you an alibi," she said, her soft voice as hard as it could probably get.

He laughed without humor at her attempted interrogation. "Yeah, I guess it does. So everybody's a suspect?"

"You tell me."

Hell, yes, but she didn't need to know that. "It's a police investigation."

"So you're not going to tell me anything else?"

He didn't really know anything else…yet. He didn't know how much Sasha knew of Nadine's past. Was she aware of the bad checks, the shoplifting? If she didn't already know, he didn't think she needed to. But who was he protecting, Nadine or Sasha? "It's for the best."

"Whose best? Mine or yours?" she asked, anger tightening the curve of her lips. Would a kiss soften that hard line?

"You've got a lot of things to deal with. Focus on them." And he had a great many other things to focus on other than her mouth, on wondering how soft it would feel, how sweet it would taste.

"Of course." She lifted her chin even though her eyes watered up again. "I have to plan a funeral for my sister. Where's her body?"

God, he wished he knew. Had the bastard taken her body as a trophy or hidden it to further complicate the case? Only the killer knew. "Ms. Michaelson…"

"Sasha," she corrected him as she set the mug of untouched coffee onto a scarred wooden end table. Then she unzipped her jacket and shrugged out of it. Under it she wore a sweater in a soft pink, nearly the same shade as her flushed cheeks. Was it the heat of the dying fire or embarrassment that had caused that? She needn't be concerned about not immediately planning her sister's funeral. She had no body to bury.

"Sasha," he said, liking the sensation of her name on his lips. Exotic…like the combination of her black hair and almond-shaped, blue eyes.

"What is it?" she asked, dread knitting her forehead into furrows.

"We haven't found her body yet."

She blew out a ragged breath. "Then she's not dead. She can't be dead. Why did you do this? Why did you call and scare me like that?" Anger flushed her face now, and she stepped closer to him, hitting his arm with her clenched fist.

Even though he hardly felt the blow, he caught her by the elbows, holding her tight. "She's dead. The crime lab verified it was her blood, and there was too much of it." Blood everywhere. Every time he closed his eyes, he saw the spray pattern on the walls, the pool on the floor… "She *can't* be alive."

"But she's missing…"

"She's dead, Sasha. She's really dead."

She dipped her head, pressing her forehead against his chest, and her body trembled in his loose embrace. "She can't be dead. She shouldn't be dead."

"No, she shouldn't. And I will find out who did this, Sasha. I promise you that." And he made few promises. His ex had taught him that the more promises a person made, the less she was likely to keep. "I'll worry about catching the killer. You worry about Annie."

She lifted her gaze, her blue eyes wide with fear again.

He found himself touching her, sliding a fingertip along her smooth cheek. "What are you afraid of, Sasha? You've had nothing to do with your sister in years. You can't be in any danger from her killer."

A little cry warbled from the bedroom as Annie murmured in her sleep.

"That's who I'm afraid of, Sheriff," Sasha said, her voice only a soft, quavering whisper. "That poor little girl. That's who I fear."

WHAT MUST HE THINK of her? Sasha wondered as Reed went to check on the child. That she was a coward or, worse, crazy? Scared of a little girl? It was ridiculous. She felt ridiculous. But she was so scared of hurting the child. Of failing her.

What should she do? Pretend to be Nadine, the child's mother? Or tell the truth and hope Annie understood? Was she old enough to understand that her mother was gone and wouldn't ever be coming back?

Sasha crossed the small living room to stare out the picture window that faced the lake. It was so close, only a rocky shore separated it from the little cottage. If the frothy waves rose much higher, the lake could swallow the shore. Sasha shivered over her awareness of the island's vulnerability. Then she caught her wide-eyed reflection in the glass, her face a ghost of a dead woman's, and she was frighteningly aware of her own vulnerability.

Counseling teenagers was nothing like caring for a small, helpless child and being solely responsible for that child's care and well-being. Her parents had been good people, but somehow they'd lost Nadine. She'd run away rather than stay with them, with Sasha. Whatever Sasha'd done to put distance between her and Nadine, would she do it again? Would she make the child hate her as Nadine had?

Tears threatened, but she blinked them away. She'd already cried once in front of the sheriff. She would shed the rest of her tears in private. She didn't need a strong shoulder to cry on. She'd decided long ago, when her fiancé had left her at the altar, that she didn't need anyone.

But Annie did.

Annie needed *her,* so she had to pull herself together. The sheriff stepped out of the sparsely furnished bedroom. He hadn't gotten the little girl back to sleep. She was clutched to his chest, a worn blue blanket trailing over his arm.

"Mommy?" she asked, her voice a broken quaver.

Sasha reached for her. Annie leaned forward, wrapping one little arm around Sasha's neck while she held tight to the sheriff with the other.

"Mommy…" Annie's breath sighed out as she snuggled against her.

With her niece stretched between them, Sasha stood very close to Reed, so close that she could discern each gold fleck in his green eyes. And with Annie clutching her so tight, his forearm pressed against Sasha's midriff, just below her breasts. She would have never considered passing a child from one person to another to be such an intimate gesture. But with Sheriff Blakeslee it was.

Even sharing a cup of coffee with him had been intimate, too intimate. The brush of his fingers against hers when he'd handed her the mug. And later, when she'd punched his strong arm, he'd held her, his strong hands touching her.

And when she'd leaned her head against his wide chest, his heartbeat, strong and steady beneath her ear, had made her want to snuggle into his arms.... It had been much too long since a man had touched her, especially if an innocent gesture of comfort could affect her so much. Plus she didn't know him, couldn't trust him.

She'd learned the hard way that she couldn't trust any man. Not after Charles, her high school and college sweetheart, her best friend, had betrayed her in the most painful, humiliating way...by leaving her for her sister. No, if she couldn't trust Charles, if she couldn't trust her sister...she couldn't trust anyone.

She should be relieved that Annie had awakened. But Annie scared her more than the sheriff. Black curls tickled Sasha's chin, and she buried her face in the little girl's hair. Then her breath sighed out, ragged, broken with emotion...

She didn't know this child. Until last night she hadn't known about her existence, but she loved her. With all her heart she loved her. And Sasha made a silent vow to her dead sister, "I'll take care of her, Nadine. I promise you I'll take good care of her."

When she opened her eyes and met the sheriff's intense gaze, she almost believed he'd heard her silent words. Something had softened in him. He didn't seem as disapproving and suspicious of her.

"When does the next ferry leave for the mainland?" she asked.

The sheriff shook his head. "The one you took already returned. That was it for the day. It's not tourist season yet."

"So I can't leave tonight?" Unless he took her back in the sheriff's boat, and maybe he would if she asked. She only carried some essentials in her backpack purse. She hadn't planned on staying long, at least not on the island.

"You can't leave this evening even if more ferries were running now," he said, his deep voice a rumble, his breath warm on her face as they stood so close.

Only the child separated them, or held them together…. Is that why she couldn't leave? Or did he not want *her* to leave? Her pulse jumped, but she calmed herself with common sense. He didn't know her. He couldn't be attracted to her. He'd known Nadine. He missed Nadine.

"Why can't I leave?" she asked. It wasn't as if she could be a suspect in her sister's death. She hadn't even known where Nadine had been living.

"You've also inherited your sister's estate. There are legal matters to attend to."

She blinked, confused. "You mean in trust for Annie?"

"No. I mean you're her sole heir."

But why?

"That can't be right. There must be a mistake." She wanted Annie even though the responsibility scared her more than anything in her life ever had. Annie was her flesh and blood, her last connection to her lost sister. But she didn't understand why Nadine hadn't left everything in trust for Annie.

"Her lawyer will explain. He's waiting at the estate. But I knew you had questions about your sister's death." Questions he hadn't really answered. "I'll take you there now." Yet he didn't seem in a hurry to move. He stayed close to Sasha, with his arm pressed against her and his breath warm against her face with each word he spoke. "And the house can be a little overwhelming."

Was it safe to go to the house at all? "Annie…"

"Her nanny will be there. She'll watch her while you and I talk to the lawyer."

"Nadine had a nanny?" She couldn't understand any of it. How did Nadine afford an estate? A nanny for her child?

"She kind of came with the estate. She used to be Mrs. Scott's nurse."

"Mrs. Scott?"

"Nadine inherited the estate from her a couple of years ago. Some people have disputed Nadine's inheritance."

"Could that be why she was murdered?" Sasha asked.

He shook his head. "Someone waited two years to kill her? To accomplish what? You inherited. It doesn't make sense."

None of it made sense to Sasha. Besides Annie, there was so much more Sasha had to learn about her sister's life and death. Her head spun with all the information the sheriff had just thrown at her.

"I don't understand…" And with him so close, she couldn't think.

If she'd kept in touch with Nadine, she would have known all about her life. And although she had no proof that her presence in Nadine's life would have prevented her sister's murder, guilt nagged at her. So much guilt…

"I'll let the lawyer explain everything to you."

He was waiting for her at the house Nadine had left to her. "I don't want anything from Nadine," she said because she'd given Nadine nothing, not the forgiveness she should have, not the friendship, love…and possibly the salvation.

"Nothing?" he asked over the little girl's curly head.

Possessiveness tightened her arms around the child. "Just Annie."

"Angel."

"What?"

"That's what Nadine always called her, her little angel." Sadness passed through Reed's green eyes and pulled at his sculpted lips. And finally he released his hold on the child, so that she settled securely into Sasha's arms. He stepped back. Somehow Sasha knew that step cost him a lot and was quite significant.

She didn't fool herself into thinking he trusted her to care for the child, especially not after her admission to him. But he was a lawman, and as such he had to respect Nadine's last wish that Sasha raise her daughter. Not him.

He hadn't said anything, but she knew he believed he should have been Annie's guardian. Last night and at their first meeting, she'd felt his resentment that Nadine had named her instead, and now she had witnessed his tenderness with Annie.

He more than cared about this little girl…he loved her.

Sasha found the courage to ask the question that had been burning in her throat since she'd met him and Annie. "Is she yours?"

Chapter Three

He never answered her question. He'd instead opened
the door to the mist and led her to her inheritance. His
evasion bothered more than it should have, when she
had so many other things overwhelming her. He hadn't
answered her.

So what did that mean? That he was Annie's father?
Or that he thought Sasha so out of line for asking that
he didn't feel she deserved a reply?

She couldn't imagine that he wouldn't claim
Annie if he were her father. But then, sometimes
people didn't want to claim things that were legally
theirs.

Like this house—the ornate Queen Anne mansion,
perched on the highest rise of the hill. Views of the turbulent lake were visible from the wraparound porch. On
one side of the house lay the town, on another, the undeveloped wooded area where the sheriff had told her
that visitors hiked.

Had that been who'd murdered Nadine? Some hik-
ers, some strangers who'd known nothing about the

woman they'd accosted? And where was Nadine's body? Lost in those woods?

Sasha had asked Reed that as she'd gazed, shuddering, into the shadows of the forest. A search was under way, he'd said. Had been since the crime scene was discovered.

Crime scene. He hadn't told her where in the house her sister had been murdered. But it didn't matter to Sasha. None of it welcomed her. The windows mirrored the gray clouds, gloomy and dark. A storm waiting to happen.

This was Nadine's house, not hers. Sasha couldn't replace her as mistress of the manor. She doubted she could replace her as a mother, but for Annie she'd try her hardest.

Being inside now didn't warm the chill from Sasha's blood. In fact, it pumped colder through her veins as she tried to comprehend everything she'd learned since midnight.

Suspended from the burled-oak tray ceiling by a gold chain, a crystal chandelier shed some light on the papers spread across the dining room table before Sasha. But none of it made sense. Not how Nadine had come into possession of the estate and not why she'd left it to the sister she'd resented since birth.

The housekeeper, Mrs. Arnold, shuffled through the set of pocket doors leading from the butler's pantry. The tray in her arms rattled as she settled a sterling silver service onto the table. The rattling wasn't caused by lack of strength; the housekeeper was a big woman, towering over Sasha. No, it was either nerves or anger that caused her shaking. As she poured coffee into porcelain cups, she shot quick glances at Sasha. That was preferable to the near scream she'd uttered when she'd opened the door to Sasha, the sheriff and Annie. "You're supposed to be dead," she'd whispered.

The fifty-something woman, her braided gray hair coiled in a knot at the back of her head, had the same disapproving look in her pale eyes that the sheriff had had in his when he'd first met Sasha—after he'd realized she wasn't Nadine. But had it been disapproval or disappointment in his green eyes? How much had he cared about her sister? Had he loved her?

She figured he and the housekeeper had different reasons to disapprove of her. The sheriff resented that she hadn't known about Annie but was named her guardian. Mrs. Arnold's possessiveness seemed to be of the house.

"Thank you," she told the woman, even though she hadn't been the one to ask for the coffee. She hadn't drunk what the sheriff had given her at his house, and she'd been infinitely more comfortable there. The lawyer, glasses perched on the end of his nose, had requested the hot liquid to dispel the chill that permeated the old mansion.

Drafty, damp, this wasn't a house where Sasha would ever be comfortable despite its timeless elegance or maybe because of it. She and Nadine had grown up sharing a bedroom in a tiny bungalow their parents had rented, which the landlord hadn't bothered to maintain. But her parents had made it home. This would never be.

As crazy as it sounded, the house itself seemed unwelcoming to Sasha, almost as if it wanted her gone. A draft swirled around her again, the cold air raising goose bumps on her skin.

But it was the only home Annie had ever known. Could Sasha take her away from it? Was that fair when the child had already lost the only parent she had?

Or that Sasha knew about.

"I can help you with the tax issues, too," the lawyer, Albert Jorgen, said as he dumped some sugar cubes into his cup. He was big, like the sheriff, like the housekeeper. By comparison Sasha felt small and vulnerable and totally out of her element. "There are quite a few involved with the inheritance."

Mrs. Arnold's mouth tightened, and her look turned into a glare. She was obviously one of those who had disputed Nadine's inheritance. Sasha could almost feel the woman's hatred, but was it directed at her or Nadine?

She shivered and glanced toward Sheriff Blakeslee. He stood at the window, looking out where Annie played on the lawn with the young nanny. Even as his presence unsettled her nerves, his vigilance eased Sasha's fear. Whatever the reason for his attachment to the child, he'd ensure her safety. If she stayed on Sunset Island...

"Um, I need to think about all of this," Sasha said, falling back on the advice she always gave the kids at the high school. *Don't make any decisions without thinking them through beforehand.* She couldn't make a decision today, now, about whether or not to accept this inheritance. She wanted Annie, but she didn't want the house, didn't even understand how it had come to belong to her sister. There seemed to be confusion surrounding that, and Sasha needed to know the particulars before she could make any decision.

"What's to think about, Ms. Michaelson?" the lawyer asked, studying her over his glasses, his dark eyes narrowed. He wasn't much older than her, but either his job or his life had aged him and given him an air of maturity that she hoped to possess someday.

Maybe she'd had too much thrown at her, but she couldn't make a decision with any confidence right now. Confidence in herself or in Nadine. If the estate were legally Nadine's, then she should keep it…for Annie. But if it truly didn't belong to her…

Mrs. Arnold fiddled with the cups on the tray, stalling her exit as she blatantly eavesdropped, wanting to hear Sasha's decision, too. But Sasha wasn't about to make one, not in her current condition of running on little sleep and too much emotion. And not until she had more information.

"Ms. Michaelson," the lawyer continued, "I made a special trip over from the mainland with the intent of settling your sister's estate—"

"Give her a break, Jorgen," the sheriff said, his voice harsh. "She has a lot to absorb. Give her what she asked for, time to think."

A flush stole into the lawyer's pale face. "Of course. I'm sorry, Ms. Michaelson. I understand that you're dealing with the tragic death of your sister. I shouldn't have pushed. Of course, this—" he gestured at the papers spread across the table "—can wait."

"It's going to have to," she said.

While not unappreciative of the sheriff's support, it had been unnecessary. She hadn't been about to let the lawyer coerce her into agreeing to anything at the moment. She was too tired…both physically and emotionally.

The lawyer nodded, then cautioned, "It can't wait too long, though."

Anger flashed at his warning. "Is there a time limit on the inheritance?" she asked.

He shook his head. "No. The limit is on the cash account used to pay the expenses for the estate."

"What are you saying?" the sheriff asked, his full attention on the lawyer.

Albert Jorgen sighed. "I guess you need to know this, Ms. Michaelson. The house is *it*."

The housekeeper snorted. "That woman got everything from Mrs. Scott. There was money. A lot."

"*Was,*" the lawyer admitted. "It's gone."

"In two years?" Outrage reddened the older woman's face, and she turned another fierce glare on Sasha.

The sheriff cleared his throat, and the housekeeper turned away and walked back through the pocket doors, closing them but for a small crack, through which Sasha had no doubt she intended to eavesdrop.

Then Reed turned his gaze on her, his green eyes unreadable. "I need to talk to you about this, Jorgen. Alone."

Sasha could understand excluding the housekeeper from the private discussion. But not her. She'd already been excluded from too much of Nadine's life. And it was Annie's future. "I need to know this, too."

The lawyer agreed, "She does. She needs to know there's no money to run this place much longer."

"How long?" she asked.

"Everything and everyone was paid through the end of the month. After that…"

After that she had to either tap into her personal savings, which weren't substantial, due to her modest salary. Or she had to sell. Now she understood why Nadine had left her the house.

"Is Mrs. Arnold right? Was there a lot of money?" Reed asked.

The lawyer's round face flushed. "Reed, client confidentiality—"

"Be damned," Reed interrupted. "Nadine's dead. It might help me find her killer…." His voice trailed off, his gaze going to Sasha.

She shivered. So he didn't think a stranger had murdered her sister.

"Well, you're the lawman. There was a substantial amount of money. I can't remember exactly how much. I didn't bring Mrs. Scott's file with me."

"I want your records," the sheriff said. "And any other information you can find out about Nadine's finances. I want to know where the money's gone."

The lawyer shrugged, and his too-small suit jacket bunched around his shoulders. "She was a young woman with expensive tastes."

"She never left the island, Jorgen. I want to know where her money went."

To her killer. Is that what he thought?

She shivered again at thoughts of her sister's murder but also of her sister's life and how big a part the sheriff had played in it. He seemed to know Nadine very well. Intimately?

Back at his house, he'd touched her, his hands on her arms. Had those big hands touched her sister? Had they held Nadine as Sasha wished he would hold her?

But she had no right, no basis, for that wish, just weakness. And now that she was fully responsible for a small child, she couldn't afford any weakness or distraction.

"I don't know where her money went, Sheriff. There's not much I can tell you about Nadine Michaelson," the lawyer said. "When she inherited the estate from Mrs. Scott, I inherited her as a client."

By foul means? Was that what the housekeeper's resentment was about? Nadine's inheritance, which was now Sasha's? Or at least, what was left of it was Sasha's.

"All I know is Mrs. Scott changed her will to name Nadine heir shortly after Nadine started work here. Sheriff, you definitely knew her better than I did," Albert Jorgen added, with a pointed man-to-man look that caused nausea to rise in the back of Sasha's throat.

It shouldn't matter to her what the sheriff and Nadine meant to each other. She had no interest in him beyond his relationship to her niece. She would not serve as Nadine's substitute.

"Jorgen," Reed said, his tone sharp. She waited but he said no more, neither confirming nor denying how well he'd known her sister.

Weary of it all, Sasha turned to the lawyer. "Where can I reach you when I've made my decision about the estate?" she asked, wanting him to leave so that she could think.

"You can call my office." The lawyer handed a card across the table. "Or better yet, call my cell, that's on there, too. I'll be at the inn tonight. The lake's too rough to take my boat back to Whiskey Bay tonight."

She stared out the window, where the clouds hung low with the threat of rain. She would have to call Annie and the nanny inside before it started.

"Will you be staying at the inn, too, Ms. Michaelson?" he asked.

She'd made a small decision, for Annie's sake. She didn't want to stay in a house where the staff glared at her and the resentment was palpable. But she had no choice. "I'll be here…for now."

"You're going to stay on Sunset Island?" Reed asked, drawing her attention back to him. She fell into his green gaze, into the relief there. But then she reminded herself that it wasn't *her* he didn't want to leave. It was Annie. And maybe Nadine's double…her.

"Yes." And then clarified one reason why. "I think it'll be best for Annie."

"To stay in the house where her mother was murdered?" the lawyer remarked with a snort.

Something clattered behind the partially open pocket doors, confirming the presence of an eavesdropper.

What was Sasha thinking? She wasn't wanted or welcome here. She should grab Annie and beg a trip back to the mainland on the sheriff's boat. But Annie wasn't the only one she owed.

She owed Nadine something, too. Maybe they hadn't always acted like it, but they were, had been, sisters. Twins. Not only did she have to take care of this for Nadine but for her parents, too, for their peace of mind.

"I'm not leaving until my sister's body is found. She deserves a proper burial."

SHE WAS STAYING on Sunset Island. Not for good. Very few people ever stayed for good, maybe for a few consecutive summers, but not much longer than that before they got bored with the charm and irritated by the lack of amenities.

And neither would she.

Nadine's body would be found soon. Reed had already led a systematic search of the woods and beaches. If he hadn't kept her, the killer must have thrown her into the water, probably to cover up any evidence he might have left. But unless he had weighted down the body, she would float ashore again. Eventually.

Would Sasha Michaelson stay that long? Reed

doubted it. She'd made a gesture, something to assuage the guilt she felt over the years she'd had no contact with her sister. Once her patience wore out, she'd be gone, taking with her Annie and the piece of his heart that the little girl had owned since the day he'd brought her into the world. Although the wind howled *outside* the windows of the inn, he felt its cold chill down to the bone.

"Want me to warm that up, Sheriff?" the waitress asked, already splashing more coffee into his cup.

"Thanks, Carol. I've been waiting for that stranger, the one you said turned up the day Nadine was killed."

The older woman shuddered. "God, what a horrible thing. That poor little girl. Who would have ever thought something like that would happen here?"

Not him. Not ever.

"But her aunt's here now, that's good," the woman continued. "Heard she looks exactly like her sister, huh? Gosh, imagine that much beauty in one family." She shook her head.

The island was worse than the smallest small town. Nothing went unnoticed or unremarked upon…except the identity of Nadine's killer. A couple of tables over, the lawyer sat with some of the locals. He visited enough that he was one of them, even though he didn't have a home or office on the island. And undoubtedly he'd shared most of the details of Nadine's estate with everyone. And most of the details of Sasha.

Yeah, she looked exactly like her sister…until a person looked deeper. And he'd looked. And he'd touched. And he wanted to look and touch some more. Even now he itched for an excuse to go back to the mansion, to make sure she'd settled in. To make sure she'd rested.

Sasha had a vulnerability to her that Nadine had never possessed. Or maybe he only thought that now because Nadine was dead and since he hadn't protected her from a killer, he wanted to protect her sister…and her child. But he had no reason to believe they were in any danger. And hell, he'd already admitted that what he felt for Sasha wasn't protectiveness. It was lust, plain old lust. Something he hadn't indulged in for a long while and something he had no time for now.

"So have you seen him?" he asked again, trying to steer the gossiping waitress back to the important issue. He'd been looking for the guy since the murder…in between looking for Nadine's body and dealing with the crime-scene techs. Had she only been dead a couple of days? The time had passed in a blur of concern for Nadine, for her daughter, for the woman he'd just met….

"Yeah," the waitress said but not in response to his question. "You're smart to talk to the stranger, Sheriff."

He suppressed the tight chuckle that tickled his throat. He should appreciate that he had the approval of the islanders. A murder had never happened here when anyone else was sheriff…at least not a murder that anyone had been able to prove.

Some had suspected that Nadine had murdered her

employer so that she would inherit the mansion. Despite the fact that the coroner had assured him the old woman had died of natural causes, the natural progression of her congestive heart failure, he had not been able to convince the town. And so they had always remained suspicious and disapproving of Nadine.

Again, why had she stayed? Was it because she'd had nowhere else to go?

Or because she didn't dare go anywhere else? Where had all her money gone? Blackmail?

He hadn't found anything in her past that she would have had to pay to hide. So what else was there? What hadn't he found yet, besides her body?

He needed to talk to her sister again, to find out what had gone so wrong between them that they hadn't talked in years. He had no doubts that Sasha had nothing to do with her sister's murder. He'd checked her out. He wouldn't have turned Annie over to her, legal document be damned, if he hadn't. But he suspected that she might know something about Nadine's life that could help the investigation.

Or was he just looking for an excuse to see her again? To sink into that blue gaze? To touch her soft skin?

"You're in luck, Sheriff. The storm must have brought him inside."

A tall blond man stepped into the lobby, shaking water from his drenched hair. Then he walked into the dining room. Conversation ceased as everybody studied the stranger. He hesitated.

"Over here, Mr. Norder," the waitress called out, her voice filling the hush in the room. "The sheriff wants to talk to you."

Great. If he ever needed another deputy, he'd have Carol apply. Although he didn't rise from his chair, he was ready if the guy decided to run. But Norder met his gaze and walked toward his table, conversation resuming in excited whispers all around them.

"Sheriff," the guy said, hand extended.

Reed inspected the outstretched palm, looking for any telltale wound from wielding a knife. But the lack of any didn't exonerate the guy. From the absence of any blood but Nadine's, they'd already figured the killer had worn gloves. But it was worth checking. When a friend was dead, everything was worth checking.

"Mr. Norder, Charles Norder?" he asked, verifying the name under which the man had registered.

The guy nodded, sending a trail of rainwater down the side of his nose. "Charles is fine." He settled into the chair across from Reed and turned to Carol. "I'd like a cup of coffee, too, miss."

She checked with Reed first, not heading off until he'd nodded his assent. His backup, a middle-aged waitress. He swallowed a sigh and held his first question until she'd moved out of earshot.

"Why didn't you leave the island?" Reed asked the blond guy.

"Leave?"

"A murder took place. Some of the locals left, but not you."

"I knew you'd want to talk to me."

"Why?"

"Because I knew Nadine."

If this guy was the killer, he was damned confident that Reed couldn't prove it. "How? Who are you?"

"Her sister's fiancé…"

Something slammed into his gut, sloshing the coffee around in a bitter wave. "You're engaged to Sasha?"

"Sasha?" the guy asked, lifting one blond brow. "You know her?"

Not as well as he was tempted to…but that was impossible now. Hell, it'd been impossible before he'd known she had a fiancé. He'd trusted a woman once. That wasn't a mistake he was about to make again. "She arrived on the island today."

Norder sighed and for the first time showed some emotion, regret. "I'm almost surprised that she came."

"Why?"

"She hated Nadine, with good reason," he said, fingering his wet hair back from his face. "But then, that's Sasha."

"Hating?"

"No, forgiving. Maybe there's hope for us yet." The younger man sighed again and closed his hands around the cup Carol set before him.

Reed waited until she moved off again before he asked, "So she's not your fiancée now?" He refused to acknowledge the flare of hope he felt.

Norder shook his head. "No, not anymore."

Reed expelled the breath he hadn't been aware he

held. Despite the relief, he still wanted to slug the guy. "But you said…"

Whatever was or wasn't between Norder and Sasha wasn't any of his business…unless it involved Nadine's murder. He had to forget about what the guy had said and concentrate on what he *hadn't* said. "So why are you here, Norder?"

"Came in out of the rain…"

If the guy kept being a smart-ass, Reed would hit him. And enjoy every minute of it. "Here, on Sunset Island. You came in the day before Nadine was murdered. I need to know why."

"Because she called me. She wanted to see me. And before you ask, I don't know why." He leaned forward, the jaw Reed had considered hitting now hardening with anger. "Some son of a bitch killed her before I got a chance to see her."

And he'd like Reed to believe he wasn't that son of a bitch? Reed wasn't so sure. "How did she contact you? Phone?" He intended to check the guy's story.

Norder nodded.

"And she didn't tell you why she wanted to see you, but you came anyway."

"It was Nadine," he said as if that explained everything.

And it did. The poor sap had loved her. He'd been engaged to Sasha and had loved her sister.

Reed eased his fingers out of a fist despite the compelling urge to still slug the guy. He would save his anger for Nadine's killer. Maybe it wasn't this guy, maybe it was, but he needed proof before he did anything. But until Norder was exonerated, Reed wanted to make sure the man wasn't alone with Sasha. Hell, even if Norder *was* exonerated, Reed didn't want the guy alone with her. How could Reed be jealous of a woman he just met?

WALKING THE SHERIFF OUT that afternoon had tested Sasha's sagging strength. She'd been tempted to beg him to stay or, better yet, take her and Annie with him.

Not that she wanted to spend more time with him. But he was a lawman. He had sworn to serve and protect. And he would. She could trust him to do that, to protect her from a killer.

The thought of being around a killer unnerved her. The person who had murdered her sister had undoubtedly been someone Nadine had known, maybe even trusted. Or at the very least someone she hadn't expected to kill her.

And what about all the missing money? Had she been paying someone? And for what?

Sasha was no detective. While she wanted to know who her sister's killer was, she didn't want to risk her life to find out. She would leave that to the sheriff and concentrate on Annie instead. But the little girl was sleeping now, leaving Sasha alone.

She wasn't welcome in this house. In addition to Mrs. Arnold's disapproving glances, the young nanny, Barbie, openly stared, her gaze full of disbelief. Her fixation unnerved Sasha. And so, hoping for a brief escape before the storm, she ducked out of the shadowy house, ignoring the fine mist that hung over the island. She wanted to walk in the garden that was just awakening to spring. She wanted to breathe without being scrutinized. She wanted to remember who she was and who she wasn't. She wasn't Nadine's ghost.

She had only traveled a few yards along a footpath leading to the beach when someone shouted…not her name but Nadine's.

An older man, pruning shears clutched in his gloved hands, started toward her. "Oh, my God!"

Horror twisted his unshaven features. Since he was armed and maybe a bit unbalanced, she didn't take the risk of stopping to explain who she was but whirled back toward the house. Her shoes sent pebbles flying as she ran along the dirt path.

His footsteps sounded behind her, his pace slower and uneven. She glanced over her shoulder as she reached the door on the back porch, her hands grasping the knob.

The knob that wouldn't turn. She hadn't locked the door behind her, but someone else had.

Someone had locked her out.

The man limped toward her, still clutching those long shears. The rain fell harder now, dripping off the shiny blades. She rattled the knob, but the door wouldn't budge. The sheriff had taken her in through that door, through a mud room off the kitchen.

Her heart pounded as the old man got closer. Nadine had died so violently that the blood loss alone verified her death. If she'd been shot, someone would have heard the shots. She must have been stabbed.

Fear galvanized Sasha into action again. She headed toward the front of the house, the part that faced the asphalt path.

The Queen Anne, three stories rising from a stone foundation, was monstrous. She scrambled around the porch to the front where baskets of flowers hung.

The screen door was unlatched, swinging back and forth in the strengthening wind. The heavy mahogany door pushed open beneath the light touch of her trembling hand.

Even in the gloom she could see the stain on the marble floor. Someone had gotten up most of it, but cracks worn into the polished surface were discolored, stained with her sister's blood...as were the walls. Blood streaked across the brocade wallpaper, dried now where it must have run in rivulets down the walls.

No wonder the sheriff maintained there was no way her sister could have lived through this. Even though, from the overpowering scent of bleach, someone had made an apparent effort to clean it, the stains remained. And under the chemical odor, so did the smell. Of blood.

Her sister's blood.

She'd been chased here. To her sister's murder scene.

Chapter Four

While fear of him had sent her running before, Sasha didn't even turn when the old man clambered onto the porch. She could see him in the ornate mirror above the hall table. A vase half-full of lilac branches partially blocked her view, but she watched him set the shears onto the white-painted porch railing. The rest of the lilac branches, the ones her sister hadn't had time to put into the vase, lay on the table, brown and dead.

"I'm sorry to scare you, miss," he said. "But you gave me a fright. You look so much like your sister."

Sasha glanced again to the mirror, studying her own reflection in the beveled glass. "Yes, I do."

"At first, I thought…"

"That I was her. I know. But my sister is dead."

And if she had harbored any doubt, any hope, she didn't now. Whoever had locked her out of the back door had proven their point. That Nadine was dead. And that Sasha didn't belong on Sunset Island.

The door on the other side of the foyer opened, and Mrs. Arnold stared out, her face a hard mask of disapproval. What had she expected? That Sasha would faint? That she'd run screaming from the island?

They would find that she didn't scare easily. Was that why one of them had killed Nadine? Because they hadn't been able to scare her off?

"Weren't you going for a walk, miss?" the house-keeper asked innocently.

Thunder shook the island, and lightning crackled. Gazing out across the porch, Sasha saw the waves rising in the lake, meeting the rain lashing out of the low, dark clouds. "It's a little late now."

"Yes, miss. Dinner's ready. And the little girl is asking for…"

Her mommy. And since someone had killed *her,* Sasha would have to do. A substitute for Nadine…a role she would only play for Annie.

After dinner, where only Annie's jabbering had broken the tension, Sasha played with the little girl in her room. Unlike the elegance of the rest of the house—with polished floors, Oriental rugs and elaborate wall coverings—the turret-room nursery was a bright oasis. Candy stripes of pink and white had been painstakingly hand painted on the curved walls along with little ballet shoes and bunny rabbits.

Sasha recognized her sister's artistic hand in each brushstroke. She'd taken such care to make a bright, beautiful room for her daughter. And the child appeared healthy and, except for some confusion, happy. Nadine hadn't always been a good person, but she'd apparently been a good mother.

Sasha blinked back tears as she snapped the front of Annie's pajamas closed. The first pair had more toothpaste on them than the independent little girl had gotten on the brush. Then Sasha pulled the child into her arms and settled onto the rocking chair in a toy-filled area of the large, round room. Somehow she knew Nadine had spent a lot of time here, and sitting there, rocking her sister's child, Sasha felt closer to her twin than she ever had when Nadine was alive.

"Wed," Annie said, sleepily gazing up at Sasha from where she nestled in her arms.

"Wed?" she repeated, enjoying the warmth and the sweet, bubblegum scent of the little girl.

"The blanket," the nanny said, having obviously been hovering in the doorway. The tall, blond woman walked into the room and lifted the blanket from where it was draped on the crib railing.

"Was she saying red?" The blanket was blue. But was a two-year-old supposed to know her colors?

"No, she was saying Reed. The sheriff gave her that blanket."

"Reed?"

"Yeah," the young nanny said with a dreamy sigh. "Isn't he gorgeous?"

Sasha had noticed, but she wasn't about to admit it. "He seems intent on…his job."

On Nadine. On finding Nadine's killer. But she couldn't say that in front of her niece. She had no clue how much a toddler understood, but maybe even more than teenagers.

Barbie shivered and rubbed her palms over the sleeves of her sweatshirt. "I can't believe she was killed…right in this house. This is the first night I haven't stayed at the inn since it happened. It's just too creepy. All that blood…"

The woman trailed off, maybe she'd finally noticed Sasha's glare. But she needn't have worried about Annie understanding. She'd fallen asleep. The nanny reached out to take the little girl from her arms, but Sasha shook her head. Then she rose and put the child into the crib herself, tucking that blue blanket around her.

"Blue…only a man would buy a girl a blue blanket," she murmured.

"He said it matched her eyes. He delivered her, you know. Right here in this room."

Was that the only reason he was close to Annie? Or had whatever been between him and Nadine strengthened the bond? Lightning flashed over the lake, illuminating the grounds below the nursery window. A dark shadow of a man stood out there on the lawn, rain falling heavily on him.

Sasha gasped. "Who—is that the gardener?"

Barbie leaned over her shoulder. "No, that's not Jerry. The guy's walking away now, and there's no limp. He's heading for the carriage house. It must be Mr. Scott."

"Mr. Scott?"

"Yes, Mrs. Scott's son. Your sister let him rent the carriage house from her…after she stole his inheritance."

Words of anger died on Sasha's lips. She couldn't defend her sister. She had no idea if what the nanny said and the others believed might be true. Or was the sheriff right and she wasn't being fair in always thinking the worst of Nadine?

The only thing she knew for sure was that she was too tired to deal with it. "Is there a cot I can bring in here?"

The girl shook her head. "No need. My room is right next door. I'll get up with her if she wakes."

But Sasha wanted to be close. In case Annie needed her. In case she needed Annie.

And she wished the sheriff were close. With thunder booming and lightning flashing, her fear had returned, weakening her resolve to stay. But the little girl was already asleep, the storm not bothering her a bit.

And maybe Sasha was so tired that she'd immediately drop off to sleep, too.

"Mrs. Arnold put your bag in your sister's room. It's just the other side of the stairwell, down the hall. The *master* suite." The girl's bitter emphasis on master implied that she hadn't considered Nadine deserving of the suite or the title.

Where was the gratefulness for Nadine having kept them all on after Mrs. Scott had died? Buried under suspicion and resentment.

In the morning Sasha would decide what she would do about the house and its resentful staff. At the moment she could hardly keep her eyes open. She followed the wool carpet runner with the paisley design, past the wide stairwell, lightning flashing through the stained-glass window on the landing, to the room where the bedroom door stood open. Not invitingly. Nothing about this house was inviting.

The wall sconces blinked off as thunder boomed again. Sasha stopped in the doorway, breath held until the light flickered back on.

"I hope you're not afraid of the dark," the nanny called out from where she stood outside the nursery. "The power goes off on the island a lot."

Sasha forced herself to shrug. "I don't scare easily," she told the other woman, as she had told Mrs. Arnold that afternoon. Then she stepped inside her sister's room and closed the door. She leaned back against it, the six panels of polished mahogany, and closed her eyes. Maybe not easily, but she did scare.

Exhausted, all she wanted was to crawl into bed and pull the covers over her head so she wouldn't notice the flashes of lightning illuminating the room.

She walked toward the king-size, four-poster bed. The satin comforter had been pulled back, but her bag wasn't anywhere to be found. Too tired to look for it and the worn football jersey she usually wore to bed, she walked to the carved bureau and pulled open a drawer. Silk slid between her fingers as she drew out one of her sister's gowns. When they'd been kids, they'd shared clothes. With their family's limited funds, they'd had to.

But now, even with Nadine gone, she felt as if she needed to ask permission. But she couldn't. Maybe wearing something of Nadine's, like looking through those photo albums, would take Sasha back to a simpler time. She'd never worn anything like the green silk, which reminded her of the sheriff's intense eyes.

Reed. She said it aloud, "Reed…"

It suited him. A reed could bend in the wind but wouldn't break. The sheriff was like that, strong, resilient…

Maybe she was more tired than she'd thought if she was able to weave fantasies around a man she'd just met. A man who had felt something for her sister. She didn't know a thing about him. At first meeting he'd resented her as much as everyone else on this island had.

But that afternoon when he'd left, he'd touched her shoulder and told her to call him if she needed anything. She glanced to the phone beside the bed, thinking of making that call. Instead of a card, like the lawyer had given her, she just had a scrap of paper where Reed had scribbled his name and number.

She pulled the paper from her pocket and laid it next to the phone. She could resist the temptation to call him. But she couldn't resist the silk. So she kicked off her jeans and dragged her sweater over her head. Lacking the energy to fold them, she draped them over a Victorian fainting couch. Then she pulled on the cool silk, letting it slide over her skin.

Nadine had worn this. For whom? Herself or the sheriff? Like the blanket for Annie, had this been a gift from him?

Something had been between the handsome lawman

and her twin, something that Sasha wanted no part of. All she would get now would be the scraps of whatever he'd felt for Nadine. No, Sasha wouldn't be calling Reed. She crawled into the bed and extinguished the light.

Questions swirled in her brain, answers eluding her as sleep claimed her quickly. Her heavy eyes closing, her last lucid thought wasn't of her dead sister or the niece who was now her responsibility. It was of the sheriff and his determination to find Nadine's killer.

Out of guilt or love?

"Sasha…"

The raspy whisper roused her from her deep sleep.

"Sasha…"

She opened her eyes, but the darkness was impenetrable. The storm had moved off, not a rumble of thunder or clash of lightning distinguishable in the black sky outside the bedroom window.

Not even a star.

"Sasha…"

"Who's there?" she asked, but she knew that voice that called her name in the night.

"Sasha…"

"Nadine?"

"DID YOU HEAR HER last night?"

Sasha's hand trembled against the cup of coffee Mrs. Arnold had just poured her. Some of the hot liquid sloshed over the rim and onto her fingers. She dipped them into her glass of ice water before turning toward the disapproving housekeeper. "Who...hear who?" she stammered.

Not Nadine. She hadn't heard Nadine. That had to have been another dream. Just a dream.

But then why did she feel as if she'd hardly slept, as though she'd stayed awake, wide-eyed and unnerved by the voice that had to have been only in her head....

Or had it?

"You did hear her," Mrs. Arnold said, a gleam of satisfaction flashing in her pale-gray eyes.

The woman couldn't be talking about Nadine. She hadn't bothered to hide the fact that she'd despised Sasha's twin. "Who? Annie? Did she cry last night?"

Had the little girl needed her? Instead of comforting her niece, Sasha had cowered under the covers, wishing for the comfort of the sheriff's strong arms for herself. Shame weighed on her, slumping her shoulders. Already she'd failed the little angel Nadine had trusted to her care.

"No, no, the child slept. Mrs. Scott. Did you hear her?" Excitement vibrated in the older woman's gruff voice.

"Mrs. Scott? She's dead?"

"Thanks to your sister, yes. But she hasn't left her beloved house." Her gaze softening, the housekeeper glanced around the dining room, the chandelier barely able to brighten its dark wood. Then she turned back to Sasha, her eyes hard with dislike. "You can hear her walking the halls, the metal legs of her walker clopping against the floorboards."

God, the woman was insane. As crazy as Sasha had felt last night. Maybe the house caused that. "No, I didn't hear anything like that."

"But you heard something," Mrs. Arnold persisted.

Sasha turned away from the older woman, her gaze drawn to the rain-streaked window. Dark clouds hung low over the island…like yesterday. Did the sun ever shine here? If not, how had the island earned its name? "The storm. I heard that, and the rain."

"Hmm…I didn't. I didn't think it started until this morning."

Still staring into the gloom outside, Sasha caught sight of the sheriff coming onto the porch. Rain slicked down his hair and darkened the broad shoulders of his denim shirt. Since Annie still slept, she was grateful for the company of someone who didn't hate her.

"He's here early. Wonder if he found her body yet," Mrs. Arnold mused with a disgusted sniff. "I better get another cup for him. He likes his coffee strong and black."

"He came here a lot?" When Nadine was alive?

Mrs. Arnold nodded, her thin lips twisting into disapproval. "Spent a lot of time with the little girl and your sister. Since she's gone, maybe he figures you'll do."

The older woman slipped through the pocket doors into the kitchen before Sasha could defend herself against that last attack. She wouldn't *do* in place of Nadine. She wouldn't do at all.

"Hello," Reed called out as his boots clomped

through the foyer. He'd let himself in. Obviously, he was quite comfortable in Nadine's home.

More comfortable than Sasha would ever be. She needed to get off Sunset Island, needed to take Annie back to her home. But she couldn't do that, not yet. Not until Sheriff Blakeslee found Nadine's body and her killer.

"You're up," he said, as he stepped into the dining room. "Early riser?"

She nodded. "I have to be. I work at a high school." Not that he had any interest in her. His total focus was Nadine and her child. Their child?

"Teacher?"

"Counselor."

Mrs. Arnold snorted over that as she placed a cup on the table before the sheriff. "Have you eaten yet?" she asked him.

He nodded, water dripping from his dark hair. "Yeah, down at the inn. But I can use more coffee. It's still pretty cold out there."

For Sasha, it might seem warmer outside than in Nadine's house. The sheriff's arms would be warmest, but it wouldn't be *her* he was holding. "You're an early riser, too," she remarked.

He shrugged, then settled onto the ornately carved chair across from her. "When I have things to do, yes."

But something flickered in his green eyes, a love of lazy mornings spent lolling in bed…making love. How would his eyes look then? Would the gold flecks shimmer and burn as he burned up the body of the woman lying beside him, beneath him, over him…

And she'd thought the coffee was hot. Now she needed to dip her entire body into the ice water as she flushed from the images she'd painted in her mind.

"Are you all right?" he asked, probably as concerned that she was losing her mind as *she* was. After all, she was Annie's guardian, not him. Why not him? If he and Nadine had been so close, why wouldn't she have left him her child?

"Tired," she admitted.

"You didn't sleep well?"

Not at all. But she wouldn't admit that to him, wouldn't admit that she'd thought a ghost had been calling her name. That would give him grounds to take Annie away from her. Maybe he should….

She didn't answer, but he undoubtedly knew. Maybe he knew all of it, all of her doubts and fears. He seemed to look that deep, his green gaze intent on her face. "It's understandable, you know."

That she lose her mind? Somehow she didn't think he meant that.

"That you wouldn't sleep well. You lost someone very close to you," he said, those eyes softening with sympathy.

But she hadn't. She and Nadine hadn't been that close, ever. "You were probably closer." And she'd like to know just how close.

"And it's a strange house," he added, once again ignoring her too-personal comment.

She sighed as she leaned back as much as the stiff chair would allow. "That is very true."

"You're not comfortable here?"

She glanced around, making sure the housekeeper had gone back into the kitchen. "No. There's really nothing welcoming about this house."

But then a little voice rang out, calling, "Mommy! Mommy!" And a little body wiggled out of the arms of the harried nanny and into Sasha's. She buried her face in Annie's sweet-smelling curls, drinking in the scent of strawberries and baby.

"She woke up crying for you," the young nanny said, her tone accusatory, as if she thought Sasha had forgotten about the child.

But Annie hadn't been calling Sasha, not like the voice in the night. Instead she'd been calling for her mother, her dead mother.

"I'm here, baby," she said to Annie, stroking her hand over the child's curls. "I'm here."

Annie sniffled, then sighed, burrowing her face in Sasha's neck. "Mommy…"

"Hi, Sheriff," Barbie said, turning a smile on Reed. "Poor little girl is so confused."

Sasha would have suspected the young woman feigned the sympathy to impress the sheriff. But she'd witnessed her affectionate interaction with Annie. She did care about the child. She just cared about herself more.

Reed nodded. "It's a difficult time for everyone."

"Yeah, well…" the nanny sputtered, obviously not feeling the same regret over Nadine's loss as he did. "I could hardly sleep last night, being back in this house."

She shuddered. "I need some caffeine. Do you need more coffee? I'll bring it back out…"

He held his hand over his cup. "I'm fine. Thanks."

Annie sighed out a shaky breath and snuggled closer. "Mommy…"

"So you haven't told her," Reed remarked after the nanny had shot Sasha a final glare and traipsed into the kitchen.

Annie lifted her head and wiggled around to peer at Reed. "Hi, Wed."

"Hi, gorgeous," he said, a smile lighting up his green eyes and creasing his handsome face.

The little girl giggled, probably just as Sasha would have done had he said the same thing to her.

"Tell her?" Sasha asked. "How? And will she even understand?"

God, she had no clue how to deal with a small child, no idea how to handle her confusion or her grief. If Annie were one of her teens, she would have urged her to talk it out. To share her feelings. But Annie wouldn't understand any of that. She didn't even understand that her mother was dead.

The sheriff shrugged his broad shoulders. "You're the counselor."

"High school kids, not toddlers. I don't know…" So much. There was so much she didn't know. About Annie. And her sister. And the attraction Sasha couldn't quite fight for the handsome lawman.

The light of the chandelier played over his rain-darkened hair, shimmering in the reddish-brown strands as it shimmered in his eyes, reflecting the gold flecks. He stared at her, his gaze intense. "Sasha, I need to tell you—"

Chimes tinkled, and it took a moment for Sasha to realize the sound was the doorbell. She wanted to hear what the sheriff needed to tell her, what had furrowed his brow and darkened his green eyes. Was he going to admit to being Annie's father?

But he'd stopped talking as Mrs. Arnold hurried from the kitchen to the foyer. And he didn't say anything as the housekeeper showed her ex-fiancé into the dining room. Reed's handsome face showed not one flicker of surprise. He'd been expecting Charles Norder.

She had not.

HE SHOULD HAVE TOLD HER, should have prepared her. Somehow Reed had known seeing her ex-fiancé was going to hurt her. Not that she'd gotten all that visibly upset. She'd simply stood up, Annie tight in her arms, and announced that she was taking the little girl upstairs to get dressed. Then, as she'd headed from the room, she'd turned back with, "And I expect you both to be gone before we come back down."

Norder, sweat sheening his brow despite the cold, hadn't offered any argument or explanation. He'd merely obliged her wish, the door closing behind him before she'd even reached the top of the stairs.

Reed had followed her. He leaned against the doorjamb of the nursery where she played with her niece. The sunbeam brightness of the round room was welcome when outside and in the rest of the house darkness fell as shadows from the low storm clouds.

Although her mouth lifted into a smile for the child, the emotion dampening her bright eyes was not happiness. Something tightened in Reed's gut. God, he hated a woman's tears. Hated even more when he was partially responsible. He should have warned her.

She left Annie building a block tower and joined him in the shadows of the hall. More tears swam in her eyes, clinging to her black lashes. Her voice shook as she whispered, "He can't have her. Tell him he can't have her."

"What?" Gut clenched, he lifted his hand to her face, cupping her soft cheek. "What are you talking about?"

"That's why you brought him here—to claim Annie. To take her away from me." One of her tears slid down her cheek and into his palm.

He didn't want to catch her tears. He wanted to stop them. He pulled her close, stroking his hand over her back to soothe her as he'd tried to soothe Annie the day before. But this wasn't a child he held in his arms. This was a woman, a soft, desirable woman. Her silky hair wound through his fingers, teasing his palms. How would her hair feel against his skin, brushing over his chest as she leaned over him....

"Shhh," he said, as much to his thoughts as to her. "It's okay. That's not why he's here."

Reed hoped. The thought hadn't occurred to him until she'd voiced her fear aloud. Could Norder be Annie's father? Reed had never seen him around before, but then Nadine had already been pregnant when she'd come to the island.

Sasha's breath hitched, and she rested her cheek against his chest, her tears dampening his shirt. His heart beat hard, as desire throbbed in his blood. She felt so damned right in his arms, so warm, so soft…

He wanted to sink into her softness, wanted her to burn for him…as he was burning for her. "Sasha…"

She jerked as if scalded and pulled out of his arms, her hands pushing against his chest. "Why…why didn't you tell me he was here?"

"I was about to—"

She waved a hand in dismissal of his half-hearted explanation. "You had plenty of time to let me know he was here. Yesterday—"

"Yesterday I didn't know who he was. I didn't know what he is to you."

Her voice hardened. "Was."

"Your fiancé."

"Ex." She rubbed her hands over the arms of her pink sweater, the same one she'd worn yesterday. "That was a long time ago. What's he doing here now, after Nadine's death?" Fear for Annie widened her bright eyes.

Reed shook his head. "He was here before her murder."

"He lives here?"

"No. He's visiting."

"Why?"

Was her interest only because of her concern that he might take Annie, or was she curious for another reason? Did she still have feelings for Norder? While it had nothing to do with solving Nadine's murder, Reed wanted to know. And maybe that was why he hadn't warned her, because he'd wanted to see her initial reaction to her ex-fiancé. He'd wanted to see if she still cared about the younger man.

"Nadine asked him to come. He claims that he doesn't know why and that she died before he met with her."

Bitterness pulled down the corners of Sasha's full lips. He recognized the emotion because he'd lived with it so long himself.

"Don't trust him," she advised, her voice hard. "I know that you're the sheriff and all, but take my advice on this. Don't trust him."

"You think he could be the one who killed Nadine?" Norder's guilt would make Reed's job easier. He would be arresting a stranger, not a local. The case would be closed and Sasha would be free to leave....

That last part twisted a knot in his gut. He told himself that it was because she would take Annie with her. He told himself that, and he hated lying to himself.

He had swallowed enough of his ex-wife's lies over the years of their marriage. And that was one of the reasons why he could never act on whatever he felt for Sasha. He couldn't trust his instincts about women.

What about killers?

"It seems strange that he'd stay...if he killed her," he mused aloud.

"Not if he's staying to claim Annie," Sasha said, her

gaze on the playing child. Then she sighed and shook her head, "I'm not being fair. I'm letting my…feelings cloud my judgment." She laughed, a short, brittle expulsion of sound. "That's not the first time I've done that where Charles Norder is concerned."

"What are your feelings for Mr. Norder?" he found himself asking, although the question had nothing to do with his investigation.

She laughed again. "Bitterness. Mistrust. Anger. And it's been five years. You'd think I'd be over it by now."

Yeah, you'd think. She must have really loved the bastard. "So what are you saying? You think I should look at him for her murder?"

Her narrow shoulders lifted and fell in a delicate shrug. "Don't trust my judgment or my feelings for Charles Norder. I've known him since we were seventeen, and I found out I couldn't trust them either."

"Sounds like you found out you couldn't trust *him.*" He definitely wanted to slug the guy.

"I should have known better."

Despite his intentions to remain uninvolved, Reed reached out, his hand cupping her shoulder. He offered a reassuring squeeze, but she shivered beneath his touch. Their gazes met, held, and something flared in her crystal-blue eyes. Did she feel some of the same desire he felt? That wasn't good. That would further complicate an already complicated situation.

He cleared his throat, forcing out the words to console her. "Don't be so hard on yourself. We all make mistakes, trust people we shouldn't."

She shrugged off his hand and stepped back into the nursery, maybe because she'd taken his words as a warning. And maybe she was smart to do that.

"I should leave," she said. "I should take Annie and leave today."

Reed glanced to the window, to the wind-driven rain lashing against the leaded panes rattling in the century-old frames. "The ferry won't come today. The water's too rough."

The rain fell too hard, and the wind hurled it around, obliterating visibility. He could imagine how much worse it would be on the lake.

"You could take us on your boat."

"You're too smart to ask me to take that risk with Annie." And her.

Her breath shuddered out. "You're right."

Chapter Five

She was too smart. Too smart to risk developing feelings for another man who really preferred her sister. So when Sasha caught herself staring out the rain-streaked window, looking toward the path Reed had used to walk away from her that morning, she stopped herself. Maybe it wasn't him she missed but her freedom. The pane of glass could have been bars—Sasha felt that imprisoned, trapped in her sister's house, in her sister's life. Had the voice in her head been mocking her? Or had it not been in her head? She couldn't consider the alternative; it was safer to think about Reed.

He was busy. Doing his job. Finding her sister's killer. Would he go back to Charles? Would he interrogate him? She tightened her arms around the child who'd fallen asleep there. She wanted the truth about her sister's death, wanted to know who was responsible and where he'd put her body. But she didn't want to risk custody of Annie in the process.

And she didn't want to relive the past. She'd suffered enough humiliation five years ago.

"You gave her a bath already," the nanny accused as she strode through the doorway in which she'd been lurking. The young woman was always lurking. She'd hovered on the other side of the kitchen door when the lawyer had stopped by earlier, just after Reed had left.

She'd been tempted. Tempted to just sign away Nadine's estate, let the lawyer deal with the mess and beg a ride to the mainland on his boat. She'd opened her mouth with the intention of doing just that. But then she'd remembered the risk Reed had mentioned.

If it were just her, she would have taken it. But now she had Annie to think about. So instead of a ride, she'd asked for more time before making any decisions about Nadine's estate. He hadn't forced the issue, but said he'd remain on the island, due to the weather as well as her indecision.

"Yes, I gave her a bath already. She barely took a nap today. She's tired." And now she nestled securely in Sasha's arms. Safe.

For now.

"That's my job." Barbie's voice rose to an even higher octave. "Your sister—"

"I'm not my sister." Sasha rose from the rocking chair where she'd rocked the child to sleep and laid her in the crib. Her gaze went to the window again. An eerie light cast a greenish glow from the still-hovering clouds. The rain had stopped although it threatened to resume. And the sun, hidden somewhere inside those clouds, was about to set.

She'd wanted to talk to Mr. Scott today, but after last

night and seeing him standing below this window, she'd hesitated. Fear that he might react as resentfully as the others had, or worse, had held her back from initiating a meeting.

"Are you going to stay here?" Barbie asked.

Sasha shrugged. "I really don't know yet."

"What will you do about…the house?"

"And its staff?" Sasha added, her patience worn thin by the constant battle she'd fought inside these old walls. "I don't know that, either."

"Your sister—"

She sighed, weary from more than her sleepless night. "I already told you that I am not Nadine. I am nothing like my sister."

Staring at the girl, hoping to get her message across, she noticed what the nanny wore. A white cashmere sweater, not exactly sensible for working around a toddler. But it wasn't that that drew Sasha's attention. She knew the sweater with its fringed turtleneck. She'd last seen it when Nadine had visited her five years ago. When Nadine had disappeared again, so had the sweater…as well as Sasha's bridegroom.

"She wouldn't have given you that sweater," Sasha said. "You've been through her closet."

The young girl's face flushed, and her gaze shifted away. "This is mine."

"No, it's not. I know my sister had that." But like a lot of things that Nadine had claimed as hers, it had belonged to someone else first. Like Charles. Like the house.

"She's dead."

"But I'm not. And she left everything to me." Why? Why had Nadine done that?

The young woman huffed. "Fine. I'll take off the sweater." Barbie whirled toward the doorway.

"You're lucky," Sasha added, sick of the treatment to which the staff had subjected her.

The nanny turned back. "What?"

"You're lucky that I don't want to disrupt Annie's life any more than it already has been."

"What are you saying? That if it wasn't for Annie, you'd fire me?"

Maybe the girl wasn't as stupid as Sasha had thought. "If it wasn't for Annie, I wouldn't need you. And if I see you mistreating her in any way—"

The nanny gasped. "I would never."

Sasha believed her. The child was healthy and happy, and she wouldn't be so if the girl didn't take good care of her. Or had it all been Nadine?

"Return anything else of hers that you've taken," she advised.

Hatred filled the girl's brown eyes. "You're more like her than you think."

Sasha hoped not.

"And you'd be smart to remember what happened to her," the girl added as she flounced out of the room.

Nadine had been murdered.

Had the nanny just threatened that the same thing might happen to Sasha?

FROM HIS COTTAGE WINDOW Reed could see the lights of the Scott Mansion. They shone dimly through the fog and the mist of the last of the rain. He hoped it was the last. Today's storm had interrupted his search for Nadine's body. Instead he'd spent his time investigating suspects…and thinking about Sasha. About how she'd felt in his arms, about the silk of her hair and the softness of her skin beneath his palm…

And her tears. Shed for Annie or for her ex-fiancé?

He wanted to know that. He could tell himself his curiosity was for Annie's sake, but like before, he knew he was lying.

Why did she fascinate him so much? She looked exactly like Nadine, for whom he'd had none of these feelings.

Why Sasha?

"Reed?" the voice rose from the phone pressed to his ear.

"Sorry, what were you saying, Dylan?" Dylan was a fellow sheriff of a small town in northern Lower Michigan as well as a friend.

"You've gotta get some sleep, man. You're losing it."

Tell me about it. "Yeah, yeah, you're right. I'll get some sleep."

"I can't believe it. You admitted I was right. You must be troubled."

"You know how it is." To get distracted over a woman. Dylan Matthews was one lucky son of a bitch. He had it all. Gorgeous wife, sweet kid, the respect of the town he protected…

What did Reed have? An unsolved murder where he couldn't even find the body.

"Yeah, we thought we left this kind of senseless violence behind in the big city, but it manages to find us wherever we go. I feel for you, Reed. You know I'm here for you. Anything else you need?"

Dylan had already done a lot by putting Reed in contact with his FBI resources so that the DNA results were rushed and he had proof that Nadine was dead. "You checked out Norder. I appreciate that."

"Medical resident. Except for leaving his fiancée at the altar five years ago, he's done nothing to suggest an unstable personality. But you know what that means."

With his free hand, Reed rubbed the nape of his neck. "Absolutely nothing. Some people can hide *crazy* very well."

Dylan's gusty sigh carried through the phone. "Too damned well. Be careful, man."

Reed appreciated his friend's concern. They hadn't been close while he'd been a detective in Detroit and Dylan a narcotics officer. But Dylan's move north, as much as Reed's divorce, had prompted his move to Sunset Island. If an ambitious guy like Dylan could be happy away from the city, Reed had thought he could be, too.

But he hadn't been happy in a long time.

His gaze was drawn to the window again, to the Scott Mansion where Annie was. The little girl had made him happy, but she wasn't his. He would have to let her go when Sasha left.

And Sasha would leave.

The way Charles Norder had left her at the altar. Yeah, Reed should have slugged him.

"I'm always careful," Reed said, and this time he lied to a friend.

Because he hadn't been careful that morning when he'd taken Sasha into his arms. He'd meant to offer comfort but instead he'd raised things to a new level between them, a level that had nothing to do with comfort and everything to do with the attraction between them…an attraction he was sure neither of them intended to act upon.

Dylan's chuckle echoed from the phone. "Famous last words, man. Why do I suddenly have a feeling there's a woman involved? Maybe this aunt, the guardian of the little girl?"

Damn, his friend was too astute. "It's late. I better get that sleep you recommended." He clicked off the phone, interrupting his friend's laughter.

But Reed didn't head toward his bedroom. He stayed by the living room window, staring up at the Scott Mansion. An eerie feeling gripped him, but he shook it off. He was letting desire skew his judgment. Sasha couldn't be in any danger. She hadn't talked to her sister in five years. Whatever had motivated Nadine's murder had nothing to do with her.

The phone rang, startling him as he still gripped it in his hand. He lifted it toward his ear, clicking it on. "How can I get any sleep if you keep calling me?" he razzed.

"I'm sorry…"

"Sasha?" He hadn't expected her to call. Why had she? "I thought you were someone else. Is there anything wrong?"

"Wrong?" Her voice trembled. "I…I—"

"Is Annie all right?"

"Yes, she's fine. She's sleeping. She fell asleep so early this evening I doubt she'll sleep through the night, but that's…"

"That's not why you called." Though he was damned glad she had. He loved the softness of her voice, whispering in his ear, raising goose bumps along his skin. He wanted her breath on him, on his neck as her lips slid down his throat…

God, he had to pull it together. Get a grip…and not on her.

"No, it's not," she admitted. "I…I wondered if you learned anything today?"

That he shouldn't have touched her again. Yeah, he'd learned that. "Sasha…"

"I need to know who killed my sister, Reed."

That was the first time she'd called him anything but Sheriff. God, he wished she were with him. Instead she was up the hill, at the mansion. Even though only yards separated them physically, much more separated them emotionally. He had to stop thinking about her and focus on finding her sister's killer…so she could leave.

And take Annie with her.

His heart clenched, aching in his chest. "I'll find out who killed your sister, Sasha."

"I know you promised…"

But like in his experience, promises made to her had been broken…before the vows were even taken.

"I'm sorry about Norder."

"Yeah, you should have told me he was here," she said, her voice crisp with the last trace of her anger.

"No, I meant…"

She sighed. "He actually admitted to leaving me at the altar in front of two hundred wedding guests and running off with my sister?"

No, he hadn't. And Dylan hadn't told him that part of it. "God, Sasha, I'm sorry…"

And he wanted her in his arms again to offer comfort and more.

"That was a long time ago. I'm over it."

And she sounded about as over it as he was over his divorce. All the good feelings of whatever had attracted them to that other person had faded, leaving only bitterness and regret and self-recrimination. "He's a bastard."

"Yeah, but what I really want to know is if he's Nadine's killer? Was my judgment that far off?"

Norder had destroyed her trust, not only in him, but in herself. Reed hated the self-doubt he heard in her voice that he knew was eating away at her.

"Sasha…"

She sniffed hard, sucking up her tears. Even those she'd shed that morning had fought their way free of her rapidly blinking eyes. She didn't use tears as his ex had. She hadn't wanted to cry in front of him. And he knew she didn't want to cry now. She'd undoubtedly shed enough tears over that bastard, Norder.

"I want to know if he's Annie's father. If he has any claim to her. Do you know that yet?"

He hadn't been able to find Norder after he'd left the Scott Mansion. But with the turbulent waters, he was sure the man hadn't left the island. "I had him checked out."

"But you don't know."

"No. I will find out, though."

Her breath shuddered out and into his ear. "Maybe it would be better if I didn't know…"

"I'm sorry, Sasha."

"And you haven't found her body, either."

She hadn't asked a question and he didn't answer her. "It's getting late, Sasha."

But she didn't hang up. He could hope she was as reluctant to break their connection as he was. But he had to let her go. So he offered her the same advice his friend had given him, knowing from the dark circles under her blue eyes that morning that she needed it as much as he did. "You need to get some sleep."

The line clicked dead before she could reply. And as thunder rumbled, the lights flickered out in Reed's small cottage, and farther up the hill darkness swallowed the Scott Mansion and it disappeared from his sight.

SASHA HAD NEVER BEEN AFRAID of the dark. Not even as a child…because then she'd never been alone. She'd always had Nadine, lying beside her in the bed they'd been forced to share in that small bungalow.

They'd complained about sharing that bed, but Sasha really hadn't minded. She had liked having her sister close. Then…when they were kids.

What about now?

Even though Nadine was dead, Sasha could feel her presence. When she held her sister's little girl, rocking her in the chair where Nadine must have rocked her so many times….

When she wore Nadine's nightgown, the silk cool against her skin. And when, like last night, Nadine whispered her name in the dark.

"Sasha…"

It was the wind. It had to be the wind. It howled outside, rattling the old leaded-glass windows. Thunder rumbled and lightning flashed.

And none of it sounded like Nadine. Except for that husky voice that whispered Sasha's name.

She huddled under the covers, curled up, her arms wrapped around her shaking shoulders. But she found no comfort there. She needed Reed, needed his big hand running up and down her back to soothe her.

But he hadn't soothed her that morning…when she'd cried out her fear that Charles might have come to the island to claim his daughter. Instead of calming her fears, Reed's touch had inspired more.

How could she be so drawn to a stranger, to a man who had loved her sister even if he hadn't fathered Nadine's child?

No, Reed's touch hadn't soothed; it had excited.

From the rapid beat of his heart, she knew she wasn't the only one who'd been affected by their closeness. And from the worried look in his green eyes, she knew she wasn't the only one who wanted no part of their attraction.

He had no time for her. He had to find her sister's killer. And she had no time for him. She had to settle her sister's estate and then build a life for her sister's daughter.

But she wanted him now. And not because she felt safe in his arms.

She just wanted him.

She closed her eyes against the desire, battling it from her traitorous body. Is that why she'd called him? He'd wanted to know why she had, and so did she.

Was it because she was scared and feeling as alone as she'd felt at only one other time in her life? When her father had started her down the aisle before realizing her groom wasn't standing at the altar, she'd felt desperately alone even though hundreds of her friends and family had sat in that church watching her. Instead of gasps of awe at how she looked in her white wedding gown and veil, they'd murmured their shock and sympathy.

And pity.

She'd really hated the pity. And so she hadn't admitted to Reed how scared and alone she felt. Instead she'd demanded answers that it wasn't reasonable for him to have yet. Nadine had only been dead a matter of days, and the storm had to have stopped or at least slowed his search for her body.

And as for the killer…if the person had been clever enough to fool Nadine, they were clever, maybe too clever, to ever be caught.

But had she wanted answers about Nadine's murder? Or had she simply wanted to hear the sheriff's deep voice rumble in her ear, to remember the strength of his arms around her, the solidness of his muscled chest beneath her cheek?

And she had remembered all those things and more when she'd called him. Maybe it was a good thing the line had gone dead in the storm. Otherwise she might have made a fool of herself.

She might have betrayed her attraction to him.

Or worse, she might have admitted that she heard a voice in the night, that she heard her dead twin calling her name.

"Sasha…"

She flattened her palms against her ears, trying to shut out the ghostly voice.

"No, go away," she whispered back, willing sleep to claim her. "Please, Nadine, leave me alone…"

"No…" the voice moaned.

A shudder wracked her body. Had she lost her mind? She was arguing with a ghost.

Or was Nadine a ghost? Was she really dead? No one had found her body, just the blood.

Nadine had hated her enough to steal away her fiancé on her wedding day. Did she hate her enough to drive her out of her mind?

Sasha wouldn't make it easy for her. She dropped her

hands from her ears. And as she did, she heard another cry. Annie's. She'd already figured the child wouldn't sleep through the night. Despite how soundly she usually slept, the storm must have awakened her.

"Sasha…"

She ignored the whisper as she kicked back the covers. Because of the dark, she didn't bother searching for a robe. And maybe a little of the coward remained, restraining her from opening the closet doors. Instead she pulled open the bedroom door from where it had stood ajar so that she'd be able to hear Annie.

The nanny was closer. She was the one who always responded when Annie awakened. But Sasha had to go to the little girl, not because Annie needed her but because she needed Annie. Needed to hold her, to soothe her, to soothe herself.

Her bare feet padded against the worn, Oriental runner as she felt her way down the hall toward the room in the turret, the nursery. That door stood open. Lightning flashed through the window, illuminating the room where the child now slept peacefully again in the crib. And in the corner the rocker moved to and fro, as if someone sat in it.

She had caught that movement earlier today when soft humming had drawn her into the nursery. But then, in the greenish light that was all the storm had allowed, she'd thought the nanny had just vacated the room… and the chair. When she'd later asked the girl about it, she had denied being in the room at the time.

But she doubted the young nurse told the truth all

that often. And earlier, her thinly veiled threat had unnerved Sasha.

Maybe that was why she'd called Reed, to ask him about Barbie, to have him investigate the young woman. She needed to tell him about her threat.

But she couldn't tell him about this. Not about this voice….

"Sasha…"

Tears burned behind her eyes. Emotion tearing at her, she asked, "Why, Nadine? Why are you doing this? Why do you hate me so? I loved you…as much as you let me. Why?"

But the whisper didn't answer her impassioned plea for understanding.

The rocker stopped moving.

Outside the storm died down.

All she heard now was the soft, even breathing of Nadine's sleeping child.

She wasn't needed here. The blue blanket had even been tucked under Annie's chin, so that the satin edge rubbed against her skin, the way she liked it.

Annie was fine.

Sasha was the one who needed sleep. That had to be it. Lack of sleep was making her crazy.

Wasn't sleep deprivation a method of torture? It would take more than this to break her spirit or her mind.

When the whisper called out again, urgency in Nadine's raspy voice, Sasha shut her out. She wouldn't listen.

She backed out of the nursery, heading down the hall toward Nadine's room. But as she passed the stairs, something moved in the deep shadows. Before she could turn around, strong hands struck her back, pushing her toward the hardwood steps. She threw her arms out, clutching, but found only empty air.

Chapter Six

"I didn't hit my head," Sasha said, anger sharpening her soft voice. "I caught the railing."

And she had the swollen wrist to prove it. The faint glow of dawn filtered through the blinds, barely illuminating the redness of her wrist and the paleness of her frightened face.

Reed pressed a pack of melting ice against the bruised skin, anger causing his fingers to shake some. "I believe you, Sasha. I believe that someone pushed you."

And he wanted to push that person back…behind a cell door. Or worse.

"You're the only one, then." She closed her eyes, leaning her head back against the pillow. He'd talked her into resting while he searched the house using a flashlight, since the blackout continued. But he doubted she'd closed her eyes until now. "Did you find anything?"

He stalled for time. "What do you mean?"

"You said you were looking for signs of a break-in, of an intruder."

Despite her objections, he had searched. It wasn't that she'd been afraid of his leaving her, or at least that wasn't what she'd admitted to. She didn't believe an intruder had pushed her.

And neither did he.

"You didn't find anything." She correctly interpreted his silence even though she kept her eyes closed. "I knew you wouldn't."

"A break-in wasn't necessary, Sasha. The back door wasn't locked. Mrs. Arnold admitted that it never is." So that Mr. Scott could use the kitchen, or any other part of the house that should have been his. He'd gotten that much of a confession out of the closemouthed housekeeper.

"Nobody came in from outside," she said, her voice breaking with either fear or outrage. Maybe both. "The person who pushed me was already inside."

When he'd questioned the staff, he'd picked up on their disbelief of her claim that someone had pushed her. And he'd also picked up on their dislike of Sasha. They'd disliked Nadine, too. He'd only known these people a couple years. He didn't know what they were capable of.

Murder? Pushing someone down a flight of stairs?

Or trying to.

Sasha had caught herself.

Thank God.

He released the breath he'd held since Sasha had called his cell phone from hers. Since the power was still out, candles lit the rest of the house. But the one on her bedside had already burned out. Only the green-ish light of dawn slanted across the bed where she lay. "The important thing is that you're all right."

But was she? She'd made some pretty wild accusations when he'd first arrived at the mansion.

She opened her eyes and trained her crystal-blue gaze on him. "You've got that look again," she said. "Like you think I took a blow to the head. I didn't."

"But you said…" That Nadine had pushed her.

Some color finally flushed into her face, which had been nearly as pale as the white silk pillowcase beneath her head. "I know what I said. I'm telling you she's not dead. This is a trick."

He brushed a lock of glossy ebony hair back from her cheek. "An FBI lab processed the crime scene, Sasha. That's how I got the results so quickly. And I don't doubt their accuracy. She's dead. I believe you were pushed, but Nadine wasn't the one who pushed you."

She caught his hand, holding it to her face. "I know you don't know me, but you have to believe me, Reed. I'm really not crazy."

"I know that." And he did. Nadine wouldn't have trusted her with her daughter if she'd thought that. She'd loved Annie too much. While he might not trust his own instincts about women, he trusted a mother's instincts regarding the well-being of her child. That and his background check of Sasha were the only reasons he'd been able to turn Annie over to an aunt she'd never met.

Her fingers threaded through his, and her eyes moistened with unshed tears. "I hear her."

Just the hint of her tears had his gut tightening. "You what?"

"I hear *her*." She shook her head, tumbling her silky hair around the hand and wrist he still held to her face. "Oh, God, that sounds so crazy. I know you think you have evidence of her death—"

"Sasha, I *do* have evidence. Irrefutable evidence. Your sister is dead." Annie's mother. His friend. He hated it and, like Sasha, he'd rather believe it wasn't true.

"No, until I see her body I won't believe it. She's alive, Reed."

She wasn't the first victim's family member to refuse to accept a loved one's death. Maybe the guilt she felt over her estrangement from her sister was so extreme that she couldn't accept that Nadine had gone before they made amends.

He stroked his fingers over her silky cheek. "I'm sorry, Sasha…"

She closed her eyes, but one tear slid through her thick lashes. "You don't believe me."

"Sasha…"

"With how you felt about Nadine, I would think you'd be happy that she's alive."

"None of this makes any sense." He wasn't even going to question what she thought he had felt about Nadine. He hadn't always been sure about that himself. "You think she faked her death? Why? What could she gain from that?"

"You don't understand," she said, as she blinked furiously at her tears. "She hated—hates me."

He had no siblings, just parents who thought he was crazy for moving farther north as they had retired to Florida. He didn't understand sibling rivalry. "This isn't like stealing a fiancé."

Sasha nodded. "I know. It doesn't make sense…."

She blinked a few more times, clearing away her tears but not the sleep. Had she gotten any sleep since he'd called her with the tragic news of Nadine's death? He doubted it.

"I don't know what Nadine felt about you. She never mentioned you." But maybe once. Once when she'd flirted, as Nadine had always flirted, she'd made a remark that Reed needed a woman just like her but *not* her. Had she been talking about Sasha?

He'd laughed off her comment then. He'd had a woman turn his life upside down once, and he wasn't willing to take that risk again.

Not then.

Not now.

Not even for Sasha.

"Nadine would never have put Annie through this. She loved her daughter, Sasha. And she left her daughter in your care. I don't think she hated you." He lifted his other hand from the ice pack he had on her wrist, cupping her face with that hand, too. "I think she loved you."

She shivered. "Your hand's cold."

She moved her face, brushing her lips across his palm. Then shock filled her eyes over her impulse.

He grinned, touched by her gesture. And aroused. Desire coursed through his body, tautening his muscles, as her breath teased his skin. He'd wanted her kiss since the moment he'd met her.

He tipped her chin up as he leaned forward, trapped in her crystal-blue gaze…until she closed her eyes. Then he moved closer, his mouth touching hers, so soft, so sweet. A sigh slipped out of her lips, feathering against his, and he breathed in her sweetness.

His gut clenched as desire gripped him. He deepened the kiss, then stroked his fingers along her jaw to her throat. Her skin was as silky as the mound of pillows against which she lay. And her flavor…

His tongue dipped inside her mouth, sliding along the soft inside curve of her lip. Delicious and sweet like an overripe peach.

She moaned and arched into him. He wanted to crush her to him, to bury himself inside her. It had been too damned long…and it had never been Sasha. But she'd been hurt and she was so exhausted she thought her dead sister had tried to kill her.

He couldn't take advantage of her vulnerability. Groaning, he drew away. But she threaded her fingers through his hair and pulled him back for another kiss.

Her lips slid over his, warm and moist, and she moaned his name. "Reed…"

"Sasha…"

He traced her face with his fingertips as he sank into the kiss and pressed his taut body close to her soft one. She arched into him, the tips of her breasts pushing against his chest even through the layers of clothes separating them.

His fingers stroked around her waist, toying with the hem of her sweater while his knuckles brushed against her bare skin. He wanted to lift the knit fabric, wanted to see her, wanted to taste her.

He deepened the kiss, his tongue dancing through her parted lips, teasing her and himself with the promise of all the intimate things he wanted to do to her…with her.

Sasha's hands slid from his hair, running down his back to grasp at his shirt as she jerked it from his jeans. Then she whimpered.

He pulled back, some latent sense of chivalry reminding him of her injury. "You're hurt, Sasha."

The ice bag he'd pressed to her wrist lay now against his thigh, but he needed more than that to cool his ardor. While he considered putting the ice on his lap, he doubted that would help, either.

She shook her head, her black hair tangling around her flushed face. "No, I'm not…"

"You are. Your wrist—"

"Reed, I think I'm losing my mind," she said, her voice catching with emotion. "Nothing feels right, but this…but you…."

And she slid her arms around his waist, then reached up, kissing him again.

He cursed his weakness, but he couldn't resist one more brush against the softness of her lips, one more taste of her sweet mouth. But one more wasn't enough, only left him greedier for more…for everything.

Her nails raked up the skin of his back as her hands moved beneath his shirt. He inched up the hem of her sweater, baring a tantalizing inch of satiny skin as his mouth made love to hers, as he wanted to make love to her….

The creak of an opening door dimly registered in his passion-fogged mind. Then a man cleared his throat and said, "I hate to interrupt…but you called me here."

Reed swallowed a curse. The man had great damned timing. "Norder."

"You called him here?" Sasha asked, her eyes narrowing even as her swollen lips attested to the passion of their kisses. Anger flared in her bright eyes and something else, something vulnerable, that kicked at his conscience. "You called him here. Again."

He had to make her understand, about Norder…and about them, how they could *not* let this happen again. But with the man listening and watching them, he could only offer a quick explanation. "I have some emergency medical training, but I wanted you checked out by someone with more."

"He's a med school dropout—"

"I went back, Sasha," Norder added with quiet pride. "I'm a resident now."

"I didn't hit *my* head," she said again, but the anger in her eyes indicated that she'd thought Reed had. And after the way he'd kissed her, he wondered if she might be right.

"Your wrist needs to be looked at," he said, knowing that her well-being was the most important thing, maybe a little too important, to him.

She bent it without wincing, but a little muscle ticked in her cheek. "It's fine. I couldn't move it like that if it was broken."

"That's not true. There are a lot of fine bones in your wrist," Norder argued. "We should get you to a hospital. You really need an X ray."

"I really need some sleep," she argued. "Annie will be up soon."

The light filtering through the blinds had brightened as much as the thick gray clouds allowed. Dawn had passed into morning as quickly as Reed had passed another sleepless night.

"The nanny will watch her," he said.

Sasha shook her head. "I don't trust her. I don't trust anyone in this house." Her gaze included Norder and him.

With the reception she'd gotten since her arrival on Sunset Island, and with what Norder had done to her, Reed couldn't blame her. She was a smart lady. Especially since she didn't trust him.

What the hell had he been thinking?

Not about calling Norder. That had been for her welfare.

About kissing her. He should have resisted the temptation. And he should have had enough sense to not want to do it again. But his lips burned to touch hers, to taste her even as her flavor lingered on his tongue.

He should have enough sense.

But he didn't. And that scared him as much as a killer on the loose.

"THINGS MOVING KIND OF FAST between you and the sheriff," Charles observed as he held her wrist, gently probing the swollen flesh.

His touch didn't raise goose bumps on her skin as Reed's did. It didn't make her feel crazier than hearing her dead sister's voice in her head.

How could she have kissed Reed like that? How could she have wanted him so much that she'd nearly thrown herself at him? Embarrassment burned in her cheeks. She was glad the sheriff had left the room after she'd overridden his objections to leaving her alone with Charles.

And he'd settled her fears about the nanny. The young woman would not hurt Annie. But what about Sasha? Had Barbie been the one to push her? Or was her other suspicion right, the one the sheriff had said was impossible? Had Nadine pushed her?

Charles cleared his throat, drawing her attention back to him. "Don't you think it's too fast, Sasha?"

It was none of his damned business what she thought anymore. Anger pushed the embarrassment aside. "Oh, I don't know…I've known him about as long as you knew Nadine before you ran off with her on our wedding day."

He flinched. "That's not exactly true."

"What?" Not that she cared. But she was intrigued that he would try to defend himself now, all these years later.

"Before she dropped out, Nadine went to the same high school as we did."

"And?"

"I knew her then."

She'd never realized that. She and Charles had only started dating after Nadine had run away. Had she served as a substitute then for the woman he'd really wanted? Had she just nearly served the same purpose for the sheriff?

At the thought, nausea rose to her throat, and she had to swallow hard. Maybe she should have been grateful to Charles for interrupting her and Reed, but all she could summon for her ex-fiancé was disgust.

"So that excuses what you did to me?" she asked. "That excuses leaving me at the altar on our wedding day?"

"No. Nothing does that. I'm sorry, Sasha," he said with a heavy sigh. "You'll never know how sorry."

"Guess not, since you never bothered to apologize before." She hated the bitterness she still felt, but it was *all* she felt for Charles Norder. Nothing else. And shouldn't she have felt something else, some trace of whatever had attracted her to him in the first place? She'd almost married him, would have if he hadn't run off with her sister.

At least Nadine had called after what would have been her wedding day, but Sasha had been too angry and hurt to listen to her sister. And the words she'd said would haunt her…if Nadine were really dead. If Nadine wasn't already haunting her…

Charles sighed. "I'm sorry about that, too, but I couldn't call you. I couldn't face you. I felt so bad about what I did to you." He couldn't meet her gaze now, staring instead at her swollen wrist.

She didn't care how bad he felt. She'd suffered enough humiliation over his betrayal. She had no desire to discuss it anymore. What she wanted to know was how he felt about Annie, if he cared enough to claim her….

She strove for a casual tone when she asked, "So how long did you and Nadine stay together?"

"Sasha, we really shouldn't talk about this," he said, shifting uneasily where he sat on the bed next to her. "I hurt you enough…"

"Yes, you did. But you can't hurt me anymore." Not unless he tried to take Annie. "Tell me. I'm curious."

As his fingers probed her wrist again and she swallowed a whimper of pain, she remembered the crazy saying, Curiosity Killed the Cat. Is that why someone had pushed her down the stairs? Because of her curiosity?

Or had it been Nadine, as she'd thought? But in the cold, dim light of another dreary day on Sunset Island, her accusation seemed bizarre, especially after Reed's assertions. A little crazy. She really needed some sleep.

He sighed. "Okay, then. Nadine and I stayed together about a year, year and a half. It was stupid. I'd dropped out of school, and we kept moving. My parents had disowned me…"

She'd heard that and had idly wondered if it had

been over the small fortune they'd dropped on the wedding her parents hadn't been able to afford but that they'd had to have, or if it had been because he'd dropped out of med school. But she didn't care about that anymore.

He went on, his voice rough with memories of Nadine. "I'm surprised we made it as long as we did. We hardly had any money. Then Nadine got caught passing bad checks…"

Nadine had gotten caught, but he would have been part of it, too. "She went to jail?"

He nodded. "She got arrested."

"So you left her there, in jail?"

Color flooded his face as he grimaced. "It wasn't like that. She told me to leave her. She had it under control. I'm sure she got out of it. Nadine could talk her way out of anything."

And into anything, even Sasha's fiancé's bed. She wasn't particularly surprised by Nadine's crime. She'd known her sister had pushed the limits. How far? Had she killed Mrs. Scott the way the old woman's loyal staff believed?

What exactly was Nadine capable of? Faking her own death? But as Reed had pointed out, for what purpose? Hating Sasha wasn't enough of a motive.

"So you haven't seen Nadine in almost four years?" she asked, striving to sound only mildly curious.

He shrugged. "Three, three and a half."

She wanted exact dates, but she lacked the most important one. Annie's birthday.

"I always figured she got rid of me because she found someone else. Guess I was right," he said, a grimace contracting the features she once thought so handsome. Now she saw only weakness in the thin line of his nose and his slightly rounded chin.

"What?"

"Is the sheriff the little girl's father?" His voice quavered with jealousy.

She'd asked that once, and he'd never answered her. But she knew him now, had seen his own uncertainty about Charles being Annie's father. And she knew him well enough to know that he would claim Annie if he knew for certain she was his. But she also knew he considered himself Annie's father in spirit, if not blood.

"I, uh…" she stammered.

"You don't know," Charles wrongly concluded. "Be careful, Sasha. Don't let him use you."

As a substitute for Nadine? As Charles had used her? She understood everything now, and maybe she owed Nadine for disrupting her wedding. Because it was a wedding that never should have happened.

But what about Reed's feelings for Nadine? Had that been the reason he'd kissed her? They'd been talking about Nadine, about how much she'd loved her daughter. He'd respected that about Nadine. Had he loved her?

"I've learned to be careful," she said. The hard way. After what Charles had done to her, she didn't dare trust anyone.

But she hadn't been careful with Reed, she'd been

needy and out of control. And if Charles hadn't interrupted them, what would have happened?

Her skin heated as she admitted to herself what would have happened. And while her traitorous body would have enjoyed it, she would have risked her heart on another man who didn't want it.

"I'm sorry, Sasha. God, how I wish things had been different. If you had never tracked down Nadine to come to our wedding…"

She'd be Mrs. Charles Norder. Why did the thought cause a shudder to grip her body? Maybe Nadine had done her a favor. And if it hadn't been Nadine, wouldn't it have been someone else…sooner or later?

If Charles had really loved her, he wouldn't have cheated…not even with someone who'd looked just like her. Or had he been cheating on Nadine with her when he'd been her boyfriend, then fiancé, all those years?

"I've come to accept that things worked out for the best," she said as relief lightened her heart.

"And you think the sheriff is that?" he asked, his voice tight. "The best?"

Maybe not the best but at least a better man than Charles Norder, her former fiancé. "No, I was talking about me. I'm better off."

She swallowed the hysterical laugh that rose to her throat. Better off?

She heard her dead sister's voice calling her name and had been pushed down the stairs the night before. But she would be better off, once she left the dangers and temptations of Sunset Island.

"What about you, Charles?"

"Oh, Sasha, if I had it to do all over again—"

"No." She didn't want a declaration of love or anything else from this man. "I meant, why are you here? Nadine called you. I know that much."

"The sheriff told you." Resentment contorted his face, stealing any trace of handsomeness from it. She'd never seen Charles jealous.

If the emotion could do that to his face, what had it done to his soul? Eaten away at it, leaving him a killer?

She shivered and realized that Reed had been right to not want to leave her alone with Charles. She'd thought, hoped, that he'd been driven by jealousy. But now she knew it was more protectiveness, which was part of his job, than any feelings he might have started developing for her.

He didn't even know her.

Like she'd never really known Charles. But even though she was alone with a possible killer, she had to ask, "Did you do it? Did you kill my sister?"

Chapter Seven

"I heard her," Mrs. Arnold said as she filled up his coffee cup.

"What?" Distracted by the fact that Sasha was alone with her ingratiating ex-fiancé, Reed hadn't understood the housekeeper. "Heard who?"

"I heard Sasha fall."

"Fall? She said she was pushed."

Mrs. Arnold nodded, as she placed the coffee urn back on the tray on the burled-oak buffet. Then she turned back to him, her pale eyes wide.

"Possibly," she admitted at last. "She did scream."

When he'd first arrived, the darkness of the mansion had been broken only by flickering candlelight. The older woman hadn't acted particularly alarmed then, as the light had yellowed her pale features.

Foolish girl walking around a strange house in the dark. She slipped. That had been her statement, which the sleepy nanny had echoed.

"So now you believe her?"

The older woman pursed her thin lips as she considered his question. "She's not like her sister. They may look exactly the same, but I think that's as deep as it goes."

God, he needed some sleep. He couldn't figure out the riddles the housekeeper spoke. "So what are you saying? Did you see somebody push her?"

She shook her head, but the gray braid didn't move from the tight bun at the base of her skull. "Oh, no. I was in my bed. And it was so dark with the power out. Couldn't have seen anything if I was standing right there."

"But you heard something?" He'd asked all these questions earlier and had barely gotten more than a grunt out of either her or the nanny. And besides Annie and Sasha, they'd been the only two possible witnesses. Like Mr. Scott, the gardener slept in the carriage house. They hadn't seen anything either, and both swore they hadn't come up to the house last night.

"What did you hear, Mrs. Arnold?" he asked again.

She touched the sterling silver coffeepot, her hand trembling slightly. "Just her scream."

He waited, knowing that wasn't all she wanted to tell him. All that she had suddenly decided to tell him. Why? Why hadn't she admitted any of this earlier?

Like Sasha, he was beginning to seriously distrust the staff. Was it safe for her and Annie to remain with them in the mansion?

"And?"

"When she screamed…"

"Yes," he prodded, beginning to understand how

some detectives resorted to physically forcing information from witnesses.

"She screamed her sister's name."

Nadine.

"That doesn't mean…" Hell, he didn't know what it meant or didn't mean.

"That she's alive," Mrs. Arnold finished for him, her pale eyes almost glowing. "I know."

His heart kicked against his ribs. "What do you know? That she's alive?"

"You said she was dead."

"No, the evidence said she was dead." And after years spent in Homicide, he'd learned to read the evidence…and believe it.

The older woman shrugged, unconcerned. "Doesn't make a difference."

He gulped a mouthful of coffee, hoping the caffeine would bring him up to speed in this bizarre conversation. "How's that?"

"She screamed *her* name."

"So you're saying Nadine pushed her?"

"That's what she told you." And the housekeeper had to have been listening at the door to know that.

What else had she learned from her eavesdropping?

"Nadine *is* dead." But was he as convinced as he'd once been? He didn't know anymore.

"Doesn't make a difference." The older woman repeated her earlier phrase.

"So you're saying a ghost pushed Sasha down the stairs?" he asked, not bothering to hide his scorn.

Mrs. Arnold's thin lips lifted into a condescending smile. "You're a man of logic, Sheriff. I understand that. You want everything to make sense. But you have to admit that some things don't."

His eyes burned from lack of sleep, from all the long hours he'd spent trying to make sense of Nadine's murder and his helpless attraction to her twin sister. "Yes. But still…"

"Things happen that can't be explained, Sheriff. But they still happen. They don't make sense. But they happen. A lot of things have happened in this house, things that can't be explained."

He'd heard the rumors that the old mansion was haunted, possessed. Some people relished rumors like that, whispers of ghosts and goblins and things going bump in the night. He'd never had any time to waste on such silliness. So he ignored the goose bumps lifting the hair on his forearms.

He'd rather believe Nadine had faked her own death.

SASHA AWOKE TO SUNLIGHT filtering through the drapes that covered the bedroom window. The sun. Or was she just imagining that, too?

She threw back the blankets and crossed over to the window, pulling the brocade fabric aside. Sunlight glimmered on the leaded glass panels. Her first reaction was to squint, but she forced her eyes open, drinking it in.

Sunlight.

She had to get Annie, had to get outside in the sunshine. Because while the sun shone on the hill, storm clouds gathered over the lake.

After her push down the stairs, Sasha had changed from Nadine's gown into her well-worn clothes. But after sleeping in them, she felt the need to wear something else.

Shrugging off her reluctance, she opened the doors to Nadine's closet. Some badly needed sleep had calmed her fears and she didn't expect Nadine to jump out at her. But she did hesitate over reaching for her sister's clothes, her arm suspended between her body and the hangers. The swelling had gone down on her wrist, but the edge of the redness had turned blue.

Anger flared again, as it had when she had caught herself on the railing. Whoever pushed her had headed down the hall, probably toward the back stairs or her bedroom. Mrs. Arnold and Barbie had come from their rooms at her scream, but when the sheriff had interviewed them, they'd claimed they hadn't seen anything.

It could have been either of them.

Not Nadine.

If she believed Reed…

Dare she believe Reed?

She had trusted a man once before, a man she'd known a long time, a man she'd loved. But his betrayal, and time, had killed whatever feelings she'd had for him.

She felt nothing now for Charles but suspicion, even after he had vehemently denied any involvement in Nadine's murder. In fact, he'd been hurt that she had asked.

But what did she feel for Reed?

Her limbs weakened as desire oozed through her at the memory of his kiss, his mouth moving against hers… his hands gently cupping her face and then her waist.

She felt too much for Reed.

Annie was the only one she should trust. The only one she dared give her heart to…and just hoped that someone else didn't try to take the little girl away from her.

Like Charles.

Like Reed.

Sasha glanced back toward the window, toward the sunshine, then pulled out a sweater and a pair of jeans. After hurriedly dressing she headed to the nursery, but the nanny stopped her at the door.

"I just put her down for a nap. She was up too early, asking for…her mother," Barbie said, not meeting Sasha's gaze, looking over her shoulder instead. "I was told not to wake you, that you needed your rest."

Who had told her? Reed? He probably thought she was losing her mind. And after kissing him back, she couldn't argue with him. That had been crazier than thinking Nadine had pushed her down the stairs.

She rose on tiptoe to peer over the taller woman's shoulder. Through the rails of her crib, Annie's riotous curls were visible, as well as the blue blanket Reed had given her. "You just put her down?"

"Yes."

"So she'll sleep for a while?"

With an exasperated sigh and a roll of her eyes, the

young woman asked, "You really don't know anything about kids?"

Teenagers. Not anyone whose age was marked by single digits. "How long will she sleep?"

Barbie sighed again, long-suffering, sounding like the teenagers Sasha counseled. But then she was a little closer to them in age than Sasha. "At least an hour."

Sasha headed for the stairs, bathed in sunlight through the stained-glass window on the landing. At the top step, she stopped, dizziness assaulting her, so that the colors of the window swam like a kaleidoscope before her eyes. She held tight to the mahogany railing, turning her knuckles white.

If not for catching the banister last night, she would have fallen more than the few steps she'd missed. The landing would have broken her fall…and probably her body.

A breath shuddered out of her. Then she forced herself to descend those stairs, the soles of her tennis shoes touching each polished hardwood step as she took care not to slip. When she reached the landing, she glanced back up and caught the nanny leaning over the railing, watching her.

Their gazes met, held, the girl's animosity so thick that Sasha felt it like a blow. Then Barbie turned back toward the nursery.

She wouldn't hurt Annie. Sasha had seen her affection for the child. But she just might try to hurt Annie's aunt.

Again?

Sasha shuddered, overwhelmed by her dark thoughts. She needed the sunshine, needed it to wash away the darkness gripping her. Then maybe when she got back, she would tell the nanny to leave. But without proof that Barbie had pushed her, could she disrupt Annie's life any more?

At the bottom of the stairs she hesitated again. She could use the back door but then she'd have to deal with Mrs. Arnold. And despite her rest, she wasn't up for another run-in with the older woman. But to avoid her, she had to exit through the foyer. Through the scene of the crime she sometimes doubted happened.

She opened the heavy wood door and stepped onto the floor. Sunlight glinted off the royal-blue tiles, except where they were dulled by the bleach someone had used to clean up. The chemical still hung in the air, the odor so thick it burned Sasha's nose. She again noticed the bloodstains on the edges of the tiles and the wallpaper where it had streaked across it.

So much blood. She could tell that just from the stains. Nadine hadn't lived through this…if it had been Nadine's blood.

No, she wouldn't think about this now. She wouldn't think about anything, not Nadine's murder, not guardianship of Annie and, least of all, not Reed's kiss.

She would just enjoy the sunshine because it wouldn't last long.

The outside door creaked open with a rush of cool, rain-scented air. She breathed deep as she closed the door on the crime scene and stepped onto the porch.

Last night's rain dripped from the edge of the roof, glistening on the petals of the flowers in the hanging baskets. The pinks and reds of the geraniums shimmered in the sunlight. The rain had washed the brown of winter from the grass, leaving it a deep green.

"Beautiful," Sasha murmured as she admired the scenery. And for the first time she could understand why her sister had come to Sunset Island and why she had stayed. A few yards down the path she turned back to look at the house.

Mansion. And it was. Huge and imposing with exquisite detail in its trim and cornices. The wood siding was slate blue, like the unsettled surface of the lake, with accents of purple in the trim and burgundy in the brick and cornices.

A curtain swished at an upstairs window in the copper-roofed turret. The nursery. Behind the sheer fabric, a shadow stood…and watched Sasha.

Even though the spring breeze that tousled her hair was warm, she shivered, chilled to the bone. Despite the beauty of the Scott Mansion, something dark and ugly lived within those walls.

Hatred.

She turned away from the house, continuing on a path that appeared to lead toward the lake. Distance. She needed distance from the house, to think.

The path grew steeper as it approached the shore. Stones skittered beneath her feet as she bent her knees to slow her descent. This wouldn't be enough distance. She had to get farther away.

And she had to take Annie with her. It didn't matter that she didn't have Nadine's body to bury. She had her sister's daughter to keep safe. And to do that, to be alive to do that, she had to leave Sunset Island.

Stones skittered behind her as someone followed her down the path. She turned back, expecting Jerry, the gardener. If he had his pruning shears, she was going to scream again. She'd suffered enough drama last night.

But it wasn't Jerry.

This man was a little younger and broader and strangely familiar. She'd seen him once before…in the dark…on the lawn beneath the nursery window. She gasped.

"I didn't mean to startle you," he said, brushing a shaking hand through his wind-ruffled white hair. "You're Ms. Michaelson."

She nodded, although it was unnecessary to confirm what he could easily see for himself.

"I'm Roger Scott." He held out his hand, which was broad and stained red with…

She swallowed a scream, recognizing that it was paint, not blood, and that there were other colors embedded in his skin and nails.

But still, Sasha hesitated. Standing below him on the steep path, she was vulnerable. One push could send her tumbling…like last night. She shook off the ominous thought and her bad manners to quickly grasp and release his hand. "Mr. Scott."

What could she say to a man who her sister had probably robbed of his inheritance? *I'm sorry?*

"I'm sorry," he said.

"What?"

"About your sister," he explained, blue eyes soft with sympathy. "Tragic loss."

He was one of the few who thought so. Only him and Reed. Had he been involved with her sister? Although old enough to be her father, he was good-looking, charming and he'd once had money—that was more than enough to interest Nadine.

Could he be Annie's father?

"Yes, it is tragic," she agreed, if Nadine were truly dead....

Could she believe what the sheriff had told her? Could she accept that there was no way her sister could be alive, could be taunting her?

"Trust Sheriff Blakeslee."

Startled by his insight, she jerked, her foot slipping. He caught her, his stained fingers wrapping around her sore wrist. She flinched at the pain shooting up her arm.

"Careful," he advised. "This slope is too steep. Dangerous. There's a better path for walking, one with stairs, leading from the carriage house to our private dock."

"I'm fine," she said, shaking off his fingers and his concern. "I'll be fine."

And she would be once she left the island. Maybe a walk had been a bad idea. Meeting Mr. Scott an even worse one. But she had to know. "Why did you say that about the sheriff, that I should trust him?"

Something fleeting passed through his observant eyes, maybe resignation. "The sheriff's a determined man. He'll find the person responsible for your sister's death."

She didn't doubt that. She could trust Reed as a lawman. She just couldn't trust him as a man. Her heart couldn't survive another break, and she already knew her heart was vulnerable where Reed was concerned. It hammered at just the memory of their kiss.

She nodded, trying to shrug off her attraction to the sheriff, trying to think of him only as a lawman. "Yes, I'm sure he will."

She glanced over her shoulder, where the sunlight shimmered on the lake. Farther from shore, waves rippled as dark clouds gathered over the water. From the vantage point on the hill, she could almost touch the low and menacing, fast-moving clouds.

"I don't blame her, you know," the older man said, his voice as soft as the wind that tousled Sasha's hair.

She turned back, waiting for him to explain. What an odd, insightful man. But she didn't know if that was what unsettled her about him, or if it was that he might be Annie's father…or Nadine's killer.

He turned away from her, staring out at the clouds nearly touching the water. "Some people come to Sunset Island to visit, to buy fudge, to hike. Then they go home. Nadine didn't have a home when she came here."

Then why had she come? She had never been into fudge or hiking. Why?

"Then there are the people who make their homes here, on the island," he continued.

As Nadine had. As the sheriff had.

"Those people are usually running away from something," he said, and she realized he spoke from experience. He was running away, too.

Nadine had made a habit of running away. First at seventeen and then after Sasha's wedding. What or who had she been running from when she came to Sunset Island? Had that problem or person caught up with her again?

Sasha breathed an uneasy sigh as another thought unsettled her. What had the sheriff been running from when he moved to Sunset Island? And why did she want so badly to know?

But the sheriff wasn't her concern. She couldn't let him be. She had to concentrate on her sister. "Do you know what brought Nadine here? Did she ever tell you?"

Would she have had to for this man to know? His insightfulness was eerie, but then everything about Sunset Island was.

Roger Scott shook his head. "She never said, but Nadine was pregnant, alone."

"And your mother took her into her home?" Had Nadine taken advantage of that, as Mrs. Arnold believed?

He smiled, but it didn't reach his eyes. They stayed flat, unreadable. "My mother always had a soft spot for single mothers."

"You really believe she left the estate to Nadine?"

No one else did. She could tell that even Reed, despite the friendship or more he'd shared with her sister, had his doubts.

He laughed, a kind of well-modulated social laugh that lacked any real humor. "Mrs. Arnold's been giving you a hard time. Again, I'm sorry."

"It's not your fault." Until now she'd blamed Nadine. But if she'd really inherited the mansion…

"You don't know me, Ms. Michaelson. Don't give me any credit. It would be undeserved." He sighed, then pushed his paint-stained hand through his hair again. "I told you to trust the sheriff. Not *me*."

As the clouds moved in, the breeze grew cooler. Sasha shivered. What was he trying to tell her?

"SO THERE'S NO WAY, then?" Reed asked, needing confirmation. The wind picked up, messing with the reception of his cell. He'd had to repeat his question a couple of times to the former FBI agent, as he walked from his cottage back to the Scott mansion…and Sasha.

"No way. I checked with the techs, as well as checking out the crime-scene photos myself. By the blood spray, the carotid artery was cut. Several pints of blood lost. Nobody could have lived through that," Royce Graham said. The ex-Fed was a friend of Dylan Matthews, the sheriff of Winter Falls.

"And the blood matched the DNA evidence we lifted from Nadine's hairbrush?" he asked, even though he had a faxed copy of the report that stated the answer to his question, the reason he'd called Sasha and told her of her sister's death.

"You know all this, Blakeslee. You're a pro—Detroit Homicide."

"A couple years ago," he interrupted. He'd not had anything more serious than a drunken brawl to handle since becoming sheriff.

Through the phone, Reed caught the rustle of paper then a hard crunch. The Tracker, as the agent was known, had a weakness for butterscotch candies. Reed far preferred the sweetness of Sasha's mouth.

He stifled a groan as his body hardened, as he remembered again the passion of their kisses at dawn. He couldn't afford the distraction, not now, not when someone had tried to hurt Sasha. He had to do everything in his power to keep her safe, even check out a dead woman's alibi.

Along with the crunching of his candy, Royce Graham threw out a comment, "From what Dylan has said, a couple of years out of the fray isn't going to be enough to make you rusty."

No, he wasn't rusty. But he felt damned old. Sasha's frantic call in the middle of the night had shaken him. God, if she'd been hurt any worse…

He couldn't think about that, couldn't think about her hurt. The sight of her bruised wrist had struck him like a blow to the gut…as had her kisses.

But he couldn't allow that to distract him. He couldn't let *her* distract him, so he forced his mind from their kisses.

"The fray?" he repeated, his mind latching on to that.

"Fray—Detroit. Same difference."

Same difference. A long way from Sunset Island.

The wind whipped up off the lake as the clouds moved in, obscuring the sun. He quickened his stride as he headed back up the hill, toward the Scott Mansion. Hopefully, she was still sleeping, still safe…

"Royce, thanks a lot for—"

"Repeating what you already knew. You didn't say— why are you double-checking the crime scene? You got a suspect?"

"Just making sure I didn't overlook anyone." Like the dead woman herself.

"If you need anything else…"

"Thanks." But he hoped he wouldn't. He hoped to find Nadine's killer soon, before he…or she killed again.

He clicked his phone shut and shoved it in his shirt pocket. Raindrops splattered the back of his hand. He lengthened his strides, hoping to reach the cover of the porch before the threatening clouds released a deluge.

"Damn."

He'd thought the weather might give him a longer break. Now he'd have to call his team from the woods and abort his search for Nadine's body yet again.

Sasha needed to see her sister's body, needed to accept her death. And at this point, after his strange conversation with Mrs. Arnold, he wouldn't mind seeing the body, too. For confirmation of the facts.

And the fact was that she was dead.

Gone.

He blinked against the raindrops as he looked up, searching the dark clouds. Just rain. Or more? Lightning? He couldn't leave his team out in a storm, not as ferociously as the weather tended to batter the island. He reached for his phone but curled his fingers into a fist as some strange sound pealed out. He slowed his steps, listening.

Thunder?

Screaming.

Hair rose on the nape of his neck as he identified the sound.

A woman's scream, full of terror, rent the air.

"Sasha!"

Where was she? Not in the house. She wasn't that close. He listened, trying to pinpoint where...

Her scream stopped, choked off.

Oh, God, someone was hurting her.

He ran, instincts guiding him toward the water. Pebbles flew as he scrambled down the path to the beach, and his heart hammered against his ribs. Why had he left her alone? Someone had tried to harm her last night. He should have known they'd try again.

But maybe, like the staff, he'd had his doubts. Had thought she might have been disoriented in the dark, might have slipped. He shouldn't have taken a chance, shouldn't have believed that she'd still be resting.

Catching a glimpse of movement, he reached for his holster, for the gun he usually didn't bother to carry on the island. Instinct again.

As the wind picked up, the waves rose, crashing against the shore and leaving a foamy white residue on the jagged rocks.

And on the face of the woman lying on those rocks, her crystal-blue eyes wide-open in death…her glossy black hair in a tangle across her white face…and her throat an open gash from the wound that had killed her.

"Sasha!"

Chapter Eight

Sasha couldn't stop shaking, and it had nothing to do with the rain that drenched her clothes. Her hair hung in dripping tendrils across her face, and she blinked back the water running in her eyes. Then she realized it wasn't water but tears.

She couldn't stop crying, either.

Reed grasped her shoulders, but his touch couldn't heat her blood this time. Nothing could. She tried to peer around his shoulder, but he turned her away from her sister's corpse.

She didn't need to see Nadine to know what she looked like…lying dead on the rocky shore. She would never forget finding her sister's body.

"She's dead, she's really dead," she murmured, burying her face in Reed's shoulder as he pulled her close.

His arms tightened around her, and his heart pounded hard against her cheek. His voice, always so deep, was a husky rasp as he said, "For a minute I thought it was…"

"Me." She shuddered. "You thought it was me lying there…dead."

Even for identical twins, the resemblance was uncanny. Nadine had let her hair grow since Sasha had seen her last. The black locks, stained with blood and wet with rain, hung the same length as Sasha's. Her open eyes, wide and shocked from the surprise of her murder, were the exact same color. The face of the woman lying on the beach was exactly the same one Sasha saw every time she looked in the mirror.

She and Nadine had spent so little time together since childhood that Sasha had nearly forgotten that somewhere out there was a woman who looked exactly like her. A person with whom Sasha was nearly interchangeable. That could have just as easily been her lying there on the beach, dead.

And maybe it would have been better if it were. Nadine had been a mother, had the responsibility of a young child. Sasha had no one.

"It should have been me," she said.

"What?" Reed asked, grasping her arms, pulling her back and staring at her.

Sasha closed her eyes, shutting him out, trying to shut everything out as emotions pummeled her. "It should have been me. Annie needs her mother."

"And now she needs you," he said. "It shouldn't have been *anyone*."

Sasha blinked against the rain falling into her eyes. "You're right." She accepted that numbly, barely aware of him taking out his cell and reporting the location where he needed crime scene techs. After he put the phone away, he touched her face, wiping moisture— rain or tears?—from her cheek.

"I'm going to walk you back to the house," he said, linking his fingers with her. "You need to get inside, get warmed up, out of the storm."

She'd never be warm again…not after what she'd seen, what she'd thought…

How could she have suspected Nadine faked her own death in order to torment her? How could she have thought such horrible things of her own sister? She'd been dead, just as Reed had said. But because of that voice in her head calling her name, Sasha had had her doubts. Until now…until her sister's body had washed ashore.

"But Nadine…"

"Come on, Sasha." He led her toward the path. "We're going back to the house."

"I don't want to leave her." Like she'd found her…all alone in the rain.

"You have to get back to the house, to Annie. Annie needs you now," he said again.

"Annie…" She turned back to the child's mother. As she stared at her, Nadine stared back. "Who could have done this to her?"

"I don't know…"

"You promised me you'd find out. You promised me." She fought the rising hysteria, but, like the tears, she couldn't control it.

"I will find out." His deep voice vibrated with emotion, and when her gaze met his, she caught the hint of tears in his eyes. Was it just the rain that dripped from his hair? Or did he cry for Nadine?

"But," he said, "you need to get inside now. Out of the storm."

"Nadine…"

"I'll take care of her."

But it was too late. Somebody else had already taken care of Nadine by slashing her throat, by killing her.

WHY? THE QUESTION reverberated in her mind. Why would someone kill Nadine?

As she rocked the little girl, Sasha held Annie tight, snuggling with the child. The motherless child.

Reed was right. Annie needed her, and so Sasha had pulled herself together. But it had taken an effort, especially with Annie's soft voice calling her Mommy. Annie's mother was gone.

"Oh, sweetheart," Sasha said, fighting back another flood of tears. "I'm so sorry…."

As young as Annie was, she might not even remember Nadine, might not remember the woman who'd given birth to her and from all accounts had doted on her.

Along with grief, anger flowed through Sasha. It wasn't fair. Whoever had hurt Nadine had hurt the child, too. Had robbed her of the most important person in her young life.

She knew the sheriff believed someone from Nadine's past had probably first blackmailed and then killed her when the money ran out, but none of that had anything to do with Annie. She was so innocent. But next to Nadine, she would suffer the most.

"Mommy…" the little girl sighed.

She knew. Despite her young age, she knew Sasha wasn't her mother…even though she called her Mommy. She knew her mother was gone.

But if not a live Nadine calling her name in the night, who called Sasha?

Her sister's ghost?

Sasha shook her head. God, that was crazier than thinking her sister had faked her own death. Ever since arriving on Sunset Island, Sasha had lost control. She'd lost the calm, rational person she'd once been.

She was the person who calmed others' irrational fears. Until now, she'd thought no one had more of those than teenagers.

Now she realized she was apparently more like the teens she counseled than she'd thought. Especially that morning when she'd begged Reed for kisses and more. She definitely had not thought that one through. And while she'd like to believe she wouldn't do it again, she didn't trust herself.

"I brought you some tea." Mrs. Arnold, carrying a silver tray, spoke from the doorway.

Sasha jerked, evoking a giggle from the little girl. "You brought me tea?"

Without her having to ask, to order? After what she'd seen, she'd thought nothing else could shock her. But the sympathy on the housekeeper's usually dour face did.

"Yes," the woman said with a negligent shrug of her wide shoulders. "You got so soaked in the storm. You must be chilled to the bone."

But Sasha hadn't felt the cold, hadn't felt much of anything…but shock.

"I'm warm now," she said, as she cuddled the squirming child.

Annie got down from her lap, heading across the nursery to her toy box. She pulled out the blocks some-one had neatly arranged.

"But I would like some tea, Mrs. Arnold," Sasha said, genuinely moved by the older woman's overture of concern. "Thank you."

The housekeeper sat the tray on top of a low dresser, then poured a couple of cups. "Sugar? Cream?"

Sasha wasn't used to being waited on in her own home. "A little sugar, please."

"Smart," the older woman said with an approving nod. "You need that for energy. You've been through a lot since you came to Sunset Island."

Until now, Sasha hadn't thought the older woman had cared. She had even considered that her misfortune had made Mrs. Arnold happy. Vindicated. Because she'd thought Nadine evil. And because Sasha looked just like her, Mrs. Arnold had thought she was just like Nadine. Evil.

But Nadine wasn't evil. She was dead.

Sasha shivered, remembering her reaction when she'd first come upon Nadine. After five years of not seeing her twin, she hadn't thought first of Nadine when she'd found the body on the beach. She'd thought of herself.

Of how it looked as if *she* were lying there, throat slashed, dead eyes staring…

Had the push last night been just a warning or a serious attempt on her life? Did someone want her dead, like they had Nadine?

"Why?" she asked, echoing the question that kept running through her mind.

Mrs. Arnold grimaced, not realizing Sasha's question hadn't been for her. "The sheriff said you needed something hot to drink. That's why I brought it up."

Not because she'd cared but because Reed had. But who did Reed care about? Her or Nadine?

"Still, thank you for going to the trouble," Sasha said, taking a sip of the warm liquid. She tasted chamomile. To soothe her nerves? That wasn't about to happen anytime soon. Not in this house that Nadine had inherited by what some considered nefarious means.

"It was no trouble," the woman said, sipping at her own cup of tea.

The housekeeper had never joined her before, not for any meal. Sasha hadn't known if that was normal procedure or because the woman didn't like her.

"No trouble…" Sasha repeated, turning her gaze to the child who happily played, having now taken out every toy someone else had put away. Annie was no trouble, but once again the enormity of what Nadine had done descended onto Sasha's shoulders like a heavy burden. She'd left Sasha her child, the most precious thing in the world to her. Why? And could Sasha handle the responsibility or would she screw up like she had the relationship with her sister?

"She's a sweet child," Mrs. Arnold said, although Sasha had never noticed her pay the little girl much attention.

Sasha sighed. "Yes, she is." And she deserved so much more than a nervous aunt. She deserved her mother.

"Your sister was pregnant with her when she came to work for Mrs. Scott," the other woman went on.

"I met Mr. Scott today," she told the housekeeper. "He said his mother had a soft spot for pregnant single women."

Mrs. Arnold nodded as her pale eyes grew moist. "Yes, she did. Mrs. Scott was a lovely woman."

"You were very close," Sasha said, sympathy dissolving some of her distrust toward the woman. Unlike her fractured relationship with her sister, Mrs. Arnold had been close to her employer, her friend. So close that she missed her still.

"Yes, that's probably why I hear her…at night."

Sasha controlled the shiver raising goose bumps on her skin. The woman spoke of ghosts as calmly as she'd asked if Sasha had wanted sugar in her tea. "I don't believe…"

But she couldn't finish that. After what she'd heard, what she'd seen, she had no idea what she believed anymore.

The older woman stared at her. "The sheriff said

that. Looked at me like I'm crazy. But I thought you, of all people, would understand."

Because she heard things, too.

First Mr. Scott and now Mrs. Arnold just about read her mind. How could everyone else on the island know what was going through her head when she herself didn't know half the time?

She really needed to leave…before she lost her sanity entirely. "I don't know what you're saying, Mrs. Arnold," she said, then took a sip of tepid tea to wash down the lie.

The older woman shrugged again. "I don't know. Maybe I'm just not ready to let her go." Her pale eyes widened, her knowing gaze meeting Sasha's.

Like she wasn't ready to let Nadine go. Is that why she heard her?

"Mrs. Scott was a remarkable woman, very caring. She took in your sister even though she'd never worked as a maid before. She was supposed to help me." Resentment tightened the older woman's face. "Instead she insinuated herself with Mrs. Scott."

"So the inheritance is genuine then." And the housekeeper's resentment of Nadine unnecessary.

"On paper, maybe. But the how and why of how it got there is suspect. Mrs. Scott wouldn't have cut off her son. She loved him, did everything for him, even taking care of some of his…indiscretions," she admitted. "That was why she had that soft spot."

Because her son had left other women alone and pregnant? Was Nadine one of those women? She had nothing to lose by simply asking and so she did. "Is Annie his?"

"Mr. Scott? That child's father?" Mrs. Arnold shook her head so vehemently she dislodged a few gray locks from her tight bun.

"But you said…"

"I was talking out of turn, and I should have known better," the older woman berated herself and then Sasha with a fierce glare. "I was referring to affairs that happened years and years ago."

And Annie was only two.

"People change," the housekeeper hastened to add. "Even your sister did, after she had the baby. But by then it was too late, Mrs. Scott was already dead, her estate left to a stranger instead of one of her family."

Sasha had her doubts. Couldn't Annie be a Scott, too? Just because Nadine had changed, and she was damned glad to hear it, it didn't mean that Roger Scott had.

She looked out the nursery window, through the rain slashing the glass, but instead of the carriage house, her gaze was drawn to the other activity on the waterlogged lawn. Men in shiny slickers headed up from the beach. Some carried black satchels. Evidence bags? Two men carried a heavier burden, a stretcher on which lay a zippered black bag. If they were to lower that zipper, even from this distance, she would be able to see the face of the woman lying inside that bag.

Her face.

Nadine.

A man, taller than the others, waved those men to a halt. Then he walked over to them, standing bareheaded, his brown hair darkened with rain. Reed. He reached for the zipper, then stopped, his hand resting on the bag.

Saying goodbye? To his friend? Or his lover?

The scent of lavender alerted Sasha that Mrs. Arnold had stepped closer. She stared out the window, too. "Anyone could be that little girl's father. Anyone."

Not Reed. Sasha didn't believe that anymore, just like she didn't believe that Nadine was alive.

"ARE YOU ALL RIGHT?" Because Reed wasn't. He hadn't been since seeing the face of the dead woman on the beach…because for one split second he'd thought it was Sasha.

She lifted her chin from where she'd rested it on her knees, her arms wrapped around her drawn-up legs as she perched on the end of the sofa in the sitting room. Her blue gaze met his, her eyes so bright. Just naturally? Or with tears?

Sasha had cried so hard on the beach, her heart was obviously broken over her sister's death. Despite their rift, he knew she'd loved Nadine. And with love was mingled guilt for all the years lost between them.

The way Nadine had died could only compound Sasha's pain. It was as if she'd lost her twice. First he'd called her, a stranger's voice in the night, telling her that her sister was dead.

But no body, no certainty, until she'd found it herself.

God, he wished he'd found Nadine instead. But his suspicions had proven correct. Whoever had killed Nadine had dumped her body into the lake, and the recent storms had sent her crashing back onto the beach of Sunset Island.

"I just found this today," she said.

"What?" he asked, startled by her voice in the heavy silence that had fallen between them.

"This place. This room. The house is so big." She sighed, a soft expulsion of pent-up breath. "It could be weeks before I see every room in it."

Was she going to stay weeks? Something eased in his chest, the knot tied there since he'd realized that with the discovery of her sister's body Sasha would leave. She had something to bury now.

"Yes," he agreed. "It's a huge house."

"A mansion," she said, nodding. "It's about the house, you know."

"What is?" The reason she'd decided to stay? He'd like to think it didn't matter why. But it did. He would rather she decide to stay because of him.

But it was soon…too soon and too dangerous for him to have such thoughts about Sasha. Because no matter how many weeks she stayed, she would eventually leave.

"Nadine's murder," she said, her voice soft but firm with conviction. "It's about the house."

He couldn't rule it out. But his gut told him that it had more to do with Nadine's past. And the drained cash account supported his instincts. But he didn't want to bring up Nadine's sins with her grieving sister. She didn't need to be reminded of the bad times between them.

Moving closer, he settled onto the couch beside her. To distract himself from her proximity, he glanced toward the darkened glass of the windows.

"It's late," he said. And he should be leaving, heading back down the hill toward the little cottage his ex had thought so primitive.

He should go…for the safety of his madly beating heart. But for her safety, he should stay. He knew he couldn't bear it if something happened to her, if someone hurt her like her sister had been hurt.

Again the image of the body on the beach flashed through his mind. Same hair. Same face. Same eyes.

But not Sasha.

She sat within touching distance of him. All he had to do was reach out… He fisted his hands at his sides.

"I'm serious," she said.

"I know you are." A serious threat to his self-control, to the walls he'd built after his divorce.

"This isn't like what I said this morning—" she swallowed hard, and her face flushed "—when I thought that Nadine had…"

Pushed her. No, Nadine hadn't. But someone had. He really shouldn't leave her. Even though he'd posted an officer outside the door, she probably needed someone closer.

Could she need him as much as he needed her? God, he'd thought her dead….

"I know, Sasha."

"It wasn't Nadine," she said, and a little gasp of breath shuddered out of her.

"You're safe. I've posted a guard at the door. I should have done that earlier," he berated himself. "Before you went for your walk…before you found…"

Tears shimmered in her eyes, but she blinked them away. "You didn't believe me. I know I sounded crazy. And the power had gone out. But I—"

She stopped, shook her head. "I felt hands on my back."

She'd been about to say something else, something more. But he wouldn't push. Whenever he'd pushed his ex, all he'd gotten were lies. He didn't want Sasha to lie to him.

"I'm sorry," he said, knowing it was woefully inadequate for everything she'd suffered.

"I'm fine. Really. I caught myself last night. And today…"

For a moment, had she seen herself dead, as he had? What had it been like to find a corpse with her face? He couldn't imagine.

He moved closer, sliding his arm around her trembling shoulders. "Sasha…"

"Today was hard," she admitted. "But I wasn't in any danger."

"You didn't see anyone?" Not that he suspected she had. The killer wouldn't have known the body would wash ashore—as fate would have it—on the beach below the house where he'd murdered her. Unless he hadn't thrown her far off, unless he'd only waded out and weighed her body down with something the stormy waters had torn away.

"Mr. Scott," she said with a slight shudder, and he wrapped his arm tighter around her, pressing her close to his side. "He's a strange man."

"An artist," Reed said, but he doubted that explained the man's odd personality.

"Maybe that's why he's so insightful."

"Maybe. What did he say to you?" Had he threatened her? Was that why she'd shuddered?

"That I should trust you."

No wonder she'd been frightened. After what Norder had done to her, she was about as likely to trust again as *he* was. "Would it be so hard to trust me, Sasha?"

She drew in a quick breath, and he knew she wouldn't answer his question. "He also said that most people stay on Sunset Island because they're running from something. He believed that of Nadine."

And so did Reed, now that it was too late to help her. "That's probably true."

"What are you running from, Reed?"

At the moment he felt like running from her, from the feelings churning inside him for her. "Nothing, Sasha."

He'd left nothing behind in Detroit, nothing but a bunch of broken promises and dreams.

A sad smile lifted her lips. "And that's why I can't quite trust you. You're holding back."

"We're not talking about me." With her so close, pressed so tight against him, talking was the last thing on his mind.

"It makes you uncomfortable. You'd rather interrogate suspects than tell me anything about yourself. But yet you know everything about me, know all my humiliations—"

"Not yours. Nothing was your fault, Sasha." Not Nadine's betrayal, not her life and not her death. He wanted to lift the guilt from Sasha's slender shoulders and add it to the load he carried. "I know you're hurting…"

She turned toward him, tipping her face up…as if ready for his kiss. He cupped her cheek, rubbing his thumb across the smoothness of her skin.

"Reed…"

Her hands reached for him, threading through his hair, pulling his head down so that their lips met. Held. Breath caught, trapped in his lungs as his heart beat fast and hard. Desire gripped him, testing his control. He deepened the kiss, parting her lips.

Sweet. She was so damned sweet. His tongue slid along the straight edge of her teeth, along the slickness of her tongue that dueled with his. He could kiss her for days. Who needed to breathe?

She murmured in her throat and crawled into his lap, like her niece often did. But she wasn't a child. She was a woman who knew what she wanted.

At least he damned well hoped she did, because he was reaching the point of no return. Again. He'd reached it that morning when they'd kissed in her bed. If Norder hadn't interrupted them…

Her fingers slid through his hair, trailing down his nape to his back. "Your shirt's still damp," she said against his mouth. "You must be cold."

She pressed against him, her breasts soft against his chest. "I'm not cold now," he said. He was about to burst into flames from the heat generated between them.

She leaned back on his lap, sliding her bottom across the hard ridge of his straining erection. He groaned. Then her fingers went to work on his shirt, undoing the buttons. "You need to get out of this wet shirt."

"Sasha…" Her fingertips teased him, sliding along his chest, teasing his pebbled nipples. He shuddered. "You're playing a dangerous game here."

"I'm not playing," she said, her eyes bright with desire as she looked into his. "For the first time since I found—since this afternoon—I feel *something,* something good."

His hands slid down her back to her hips. "You feel wonderful," he said with a groan as he fought against the urge to take her there, on that little sofa in the sitting room.

But she was talking about shock, how she'd been in it most of the day. He couldn't take advantage. Regret tearing at him, he lifted her off his lap.

She lay back on the cushions, her arms outstretched to him. Passion flushed her face, her lips swollen from his kisses. "Reed…"

He'd already lost control. "Sasha, you need—"

"You." She leaned toward him, slid her palms over his naked chest, rested her hand on his heart. "Do you need me?"

Vulnerability softened her eyes, the curve of her swollen lips. With nothing between her skin and his, couldn't she feel how hard his heart hammered for her?

"Sasha…" He'd intended to stop before things went any further. But if she couldn't feel his need for her… he'd have to show her.

His hands went to the hem of her sweater, sliding up under the soft, knit fabric. Her stomach quivered under his touch, and she sucked in a quick breath. He slid his fingers higher, fumbling with the clasp of her bra. It had been so damned long for him….

The clasp released its hold, and he lifted the sweater, baring her midriff and then her breasts to his hungry gaze. "So damned beautiful…"

"Reed…"

He kissed her pouting lips as his hands cupped her breasts. Her nipples teased his palms. So he teased back, rubbing his palms across the hard peaks. Then he rolled them between his thumbs.

Sasha's moan vibrated against his lips. He moved his mouth, sliding it across her cheek, down her silky throat to the soft, delicate skin of her full breasts. Then he lapped at her nipples, laving his tongue over the hard, rosy tips.

"Reed…" She pushed at his shoulders so that he raised his head, meeting her gaze. "Do you need *me?*"

"How can you doubt what I'm feeling for you?"

"For me. Or for my sister?"

Chapter Nine

Sasha propped her back against the brass headboard of Nadine's bed. She couldn't sleep, and with the night almost gone, she'd given up trying. For once the house was quiet. But her mind wasn't.

For a short time yesterday she'd felt safe in Reed's strong arms, pressed tight to his bare, muscular chest. Then she realized she had put herself in a far more dangerous position than walking alone in a dark house full of resentful people.

She had risked her heart.

And now her body resented how quickly she'd come to her senses. It tingled still from Reed's sensual touch and ached for more.

After what she'd seen on the beach, an image of herself in death, Sasha had needed to feel alive. And nobody, not even Charles, had ever inspired her to feel as much as she did when she was in Reed's arms.

He probably resented her as much as her body did for calling a halt to their lovemaking. But doubts had assailed her. The last man she had been with—

Charles—had found her inadequate in comparison to Nadine and left her for her sister. So might Reed.

Had he been Nadine's lover? Sasha still did not know. Was that the reason for his attraction to her? Because she was Nadine's identical twin?

If not, then why had he apologized when she'd asked him if he wanted her…or Nadine?

Between deep breaths he'd said something about taking advantage of her. But it had been the other way around. She'd been the one to kiss him…first.

And then he'd kissed her back.

Oh, damn, how he'd kissed her back.

Her breasts tingled, reminding her of what else he'd kissed. Heat pooled between her legs.

Reed may once have had something going with Nadine, but Nadine was gone. Tears burned Sasha's eyes at the truth of that. But a man wasn't like a nightgown or a sweater. He wasn't a hand-me-down passed from one sister to another. Well, except for Charles, and he shouldn't have been.

It was better that she and Reed had stopped before things had gone any further between them. Her head accepted that. Her body called her a liar.

Dawn lightened the dark clouds that had hung over the island since her arrival but for that brief sunshine yesterday when she'd gone for her walk…and found her sister's body.

She shuddered at the horrific memory. Who would have done that to Nadine? Why?

To get the house? Sasha was the one who'd inherited it. Killing Nadine had accomplished nothing except to leave a little girl without a mother. And Sasha without her sister.

"I'm so sorry, Nadine," she whispered, mourning not only her sister but all the hurt that had festered between them over the years.

If only she could change the past....

But she couldn't. As she told the kids she counseled, she needed to focus on improving the future...for herself and for Annie.

And leaving the island, leaving the scene of Nadine's murder, would be the easiest way to do that. Though she couldn't trust Reed with her heart, she knew she could trust him to find her sister's killer. He wanted justice at least as much as she did. But was it because he was a lawman or because he'd been Nadine's lover? The question still haunted her, and jealousy churned her stomach. But she had no right to those emotions, no claim on Reed. And since she had her sister's body, she could leave Sunset Island.

She was going to leave.

Wasn't she?

TENSION TIGHTENED the muscles in Reed's neck as he passed his hand over it and headed up the brick porch steps of the Scott Mansion.

He hadn't come here to see Sasha. After last night, he didn't know what to say to her. He'd taken advantage of her vulnerability, not once but twice, and he wasn't proud of himself because of that. But most damning was that he was sorriest that they had stopped. His body ached to make love to her, to claim her as his. But she wasn't his.

And she never would be…because he'd been right. She was leaving.

He ducked as he passed under the hanging pots of flowers, blossoms dropping on his shoulders. He brushed off the battered petals, knocking them to the painted boards of the porch. If only he could get rid of his guilt that easily…and his attraction to Sasha.

He'd never been so drawn to a woman, not even Laurie, and he'd been married to her until her lies and betrayals had destroyed them. He couldn't risk that kind of pain again. If the attraction to Sasha were stronger than anything he'd ever experienced, such would be the heartache when she left.

He had come to see the lawyer. When he'd reached the man on his cell, he'd been told he was at the mansion in a meeting with Sasha.

No doubt she was settling the estate…and packing. She had her sister's body. All he had to do was find her killer and bring him to justice. *Justice.* Nadine deserved that.

He nodded at Tommy, the deputy he'd posted at the door. "Sheriff Blakeslee, I let the lawyer inside. Nobody else has come or gone."

Not yet. But Sasha would be leaving…soon.

"Good work, Tommy," he offered, working some enthusiasm into his voice.

The young officer grinned, barely able to contain his

excitement. Had Reed ever been that young, that green? If so, he couldn't remember. And today he felt very old.

Dampness from yesterday's storm clung to the air, and the dark clouds hanging overhead threatened more rain. He couldn't remember so dismal a spring since he'd moved to Sunset Island. But then, a lot of things had happened that he never thought he'd see on the island.

He preferred the rain.

"I wished I'd been here yesterday," Tommy said, disappointment dimming his smile. "How do you figure she turned up?"

"The storm. Someone dumped her body in the lake or anchored it just offshore. The storm churned up the water, releasing her," Reed explained. "I'm going inside now. You can kick off for a while. Get some lunch at the inn."

The young deputy nodded. "I can keep an eye on the stranger, if you want."

Reed wanted Charles Norder behind bars, but he didn't have any evidence to warrant it. All he had was a feeling in the pit of his stomach, which he accepted was probably more jealousy than instinct.

"It's under control, Tommy. Just get some lunch and get back here."

He had someone else on Norder, but it didn't look like the guy was going anywhere. Maybe he hoped to rekindle something with Sasha?

And what did Sasha want?

Last night, it had been Reed...until she'd come to

her senses. Or had she simply gotten scared? Had she been afraid that he would reject her as Norder, the fool, had?

Stopping *had* been the smartest thing for both of them. She wasn't the only one who was too vulnerable.

After seeing the deputy off, Reed opened the perpetually unlocked door and stepped inside the quiet house. Nobody locked their doors on the island. It had never been necessary…until now, until a killer roamed free.

Sasha and Annie would be safer away from the island. But the thought of them leaving had his heart clenched so tight in his chest it struggled to beat.

Then Annie peeked around the pocket doors of the dining room. Her bright eyes lit up at the sight of him and she toddled forward, arms outstretched. "Wed, pway with me."

He crouched to scoop her up and hold her close. For the last time?

Strawberry jam left a trail from the corner of her mouth across her cheek. A lock of curly black hair stuck in the residue of her lunch. He tousled the rest of her soft hair. "Hi, gorgeous."

She giggled and patted his cheek, her fingers leaving a sticky trail on his unshaven jaw. "Ow, pwicky," she said, pulling her fingers back.

Reed chuckled, then soft laughter echoed his. Over her niece's head, he met Sasha's gaze. "I've been called worse," he admitted.

Although her cheeks colored, her eyes sparkled with humor. "I bet you have."

"Wed's gonna pway with me," Annie told her.

"I came to see Jorgen. Tommy said he's still here." And for the moment, so was she. He ignored the curious feeling in his chest, the tightness replaced by a flood of something else…something he refused to name.

"I was just on my way out, Sheriff," the lawyer said with a long-suffering sigh as he joined Sasha in the doorway. Papers protruded from the clasp of his bulging briefcase. Had she just signed away her inheritance? Did she want to leave that badly? Did she want to get away from him as much as she did the killer?

"Are you on your way to the mainland?" And was Sasha riding with him?

"Not just yet. Why, did you want to see me, Sheriff?" Jorgen asked.

Reed struggled to remember why, barely able to drag his gaze from Sasha's flushed face. "I wanted to know if you'd found out about Nadine's financials. But we can talk outside."

All humor left Sasha's eyes. "You can talk in front of me. I'm—she was my sister. It's now my house, my missing money."

He turned his attention back to the sticky toddler in his arms. He wasn't comfortable talking about Nadine in front of Annie, no matter how little she probably understood of the whole situation. She wiggled down as her nanny came down the hall from the back of the house.

"There she is," Barbie said, touching a wet towel to

the child's face. "I think I'll take her outside for a little walk now…if that's all right with you?"

Sasha paused, studying the nanny.

The young woman lifted her chin, obviously taking offense at Sasha's reluctance. "I took her for walks all the time when your sister was…"

Alive. But Nadine wasn't alive. And Sasha probably remembered where Annie was the day her mother had died, on a walk with the nanny.

Barbie swallowed hard. "Sorry. It's just that we should try to keep things as normal as we can. Shouldn't we? For Annie's sake?"

Sasha nodded. "You're right, Barbie. We should."

Reed resisted the urge to argue her decision to leave the island and take the child from the only home she'd ever known. Sasha was Annie's guardian, and it was up to her to decide what was best for the child.

Sasha dropped a kiss on the little girl's head. "Go ahead. Just…"

"What?" Barbie asked, impatient to leave.

"Be careful."

"I always keep Annie safe."

"Both of you. Be careful," Sasha said.

The young woman's eyes widened, the resentment leaving them. "I—yes, we will. Thanks."

Sasha had just overcome another person's unfounded resentment of her. All this in a matter of days when her sister hadn't managed it during the years she'd lived on Sunset Island. It probably would be safer for Reed if she left.

"Now should we go back to the dining room?" she asked after the door closed behind the nanny and the little girl.

The lawyer shook his head. "Nothing much to tell. Nadine was draining all the cash from the estate. I already told you both that. But it was cash, Sheriff. No checks made out to anyone. She was spending it."

"What was she using it for?" Reed asked. "She stayed on the island. She didn't travel. She didn't shop. Where'd she spend the money? And for what?" Blackmail. That was what he'd suspected all along. Someone from her past had been blackmailing Nadine, and when she'd run out of money, had killed her.

"She was giving the money to someone," Sasha said, and he was surprised that she agreed with him. "But why? And who?"

"There's no way to trace cash. As I said, all the money Nadine withdrew from the estate, she withdrew as cash. If she'd lived, she probably would have been forced to sell the house. She didn't have enough left to keep it going." The lawyer repeated what he had told them the first day she'd arrived on the island.

This time, Reed realized that Sasha wouldn't be able to stay on Sunset Island even if she wanted to. As a high school counselor, she probably didn't earn enough to pay for the upkeep of a house the size of the Scott Mansion.

"I'm going to repeat my advice," the lawyer said. "Either sign off on it or sell it. Now."

Sasha shook her head. "I'm still not ready to make

a decision. I want to talk to my parents, and they won't
be calling until Sunday."

So, Reed had a couple more days.

But for what?

He couldn't ask Sasha to stay. He had nothing to
offer her. His ex-wife had taken something infinitely
more important than his money in their divorce. She'd
taken his ability to trust.

SASHA TURNED FROM THE DOOR she'd closed behind the
lawyer's stiff back. He wasn't happy. But then neither
was she. She hadn't asked him to come.

She knew it was inevitable that she'd have to either
sign off on the inheritance or sell. But she wasn't ready
yet.

And it had far less to do with getting her parents'
input than with the man standing behind her. Reed. She
wasn't ready to leave Sunset Island yet. She wasn't
ready to leave *him*.

"I'm sorry," he said.

This was about something deeper than interrupting
her meeting with the lawyer or even last night. This was
something infinitely more important to her.

He was sorry he couldn't offer her more.

Why couldn't he?

Because of Nadine?

Had she claimed his heart so thoroughly that even
after her death he wasn't free to offer it to another?

And after her humiliation at the altar, Sasha had no
desire to ever approach it again…with anyone. Maybe

that was the problem with them. Maybe they each were looking for something from the other that they themselves weren't willing to give. How selfish was that?

"I'm sorry, too," she said with a sigh, meeting his troubled gaze.

He shook his head and rubbed his hand over the back of his neck. "Sasha, don't. You have no reason to apologize…for anything."

She lifted her fingers to his face, running them along the hard ridge of his clenched jaw. "Sticky," she said, trying to defuse the tension between them.

"Better than pricky, I guess," he said, his chuckle sounding forced.

"You're not." No matter what he'd been called, she knew he was a good man. Maybe one of the last.

She licked her fingertips, tasting the sweetness of strawberry. Then she stroked those wet fingers across his cheek, in a gesture that was hardly as innocent as a mother wiping food from her child's face.

And there was nothing innocent about the way he caught her fingers and drew them to his lips, suckling the sticky tips into his mouth.

Desire burned hot inside her, melting the muscles in her legs so they felt weak and rubbery. "Reed…"

His green eyes darkened, pupils dilating as his gaze swept over her. "Sweet. So damned sweet…"

She shivered at the sensation of his lips and tongue caressing her skin and the sound of her name spoken in his voice, raw with desire.

For her?

"I won't be her substitute," she said, pulling her hand away from his mouth as she tried to stiffen her spine and her self-respect.

"Substitute? For who?"

She laughed with no humor and gestured toward her face. "My twin. Nadine. Your lover."

His handsome face sobered, his jaw tautening as he succinctly replied, "No."

Had he answered her? Had he finally answered her question?

"No? No what?" she probed, sick of everything she hadn't known about her sister…and Reed.

"No, Nadine was never my lover."

Had he lied to her? Just like Charles had? Her heart sank with uncertainty, but she laughed off the pain of his possible deceit.

"Nadine was my sister, my twin. I may not have seen her in the past five years but I knew her well. I find it hard to believe that you and she were close but never had that kind of relationship."

"We were friends. Just friends."

"My sister was never *just friends* with a man." Not even Sasha's fiancé.

Reed's green eyes glittered with gold flecks as his intense stare bored into her. "I'm not Charles Norder."

"I know—"

"No, you don't," he said, his voice tight with frustration. "It's been what? Five years? And you have no other man in your life? You've let no one else close. You think all men are Norder."

"That's not—" She couldn't utter the lie. It was true, very true.

She couldn't defend herself, couldn't defend her cowardice, so she just wrapped her arms around her midriff for comfort. The silence, broken only by the creaking of the old house, stretched between them.

Reed sighed, a ragged expulsion of breath. "I know how it is, Sasha. I was married once."

She turned toward him as shock rippled through her. He'd been married. And she'd been jealous of whatever feelings he'd had for Nadine? Her stomach churned with what she now recognized as a petty emotion.

She waited for him to continue, resisting the urge to reach out to him. She could tell his marriage, if it had started happy, had not ended that way.

"That's part of why nothing happened between me and your sister," he said. He ran his hand over the back of his neck again. "Maybe Roger Scott had something, with what he said about Sunset Island."

"That people come here to run away from their problems," she remembered. She had wondered what Reed had been running from. Now she knew.

"I'd had the cottage here for years. But I didn't move here until after the divorce. A very bitter divorce."

He hadn't had to tell her that. She could feel his pain, even now, years later. And while she wanted to press for details, she didn't want to put either of them through that.

He went on, "I was never really attracted to Nadine in that way. I guess I just wasn't ready to start anything with anyone."

"And now?" She bit her lip the minute she asked the question. Would she never learn to stop humiliating herself?

He touched her face, running his thumb over her bottom lip. "Don't…" he groaned. "Let me…"

He lowered his head, then nibbled at her lips. "Sasha…"

He sighed, leaning his forehead against hers. "I'm probably still not ready, but I can't seem to help myself with you."

"Then let me help you," she said, taking his hand in hers to tug him toward the stairs. She probably wasn't ready either, but she couldn't fight her feelings for him any longer.

He followed her up the steps that just a couple nights ago someone had tried to push her down. But she wasn't worried now, wasn't a bit dizzy. For the first time since she'd arrived on the island, she knew what she was doing.

Light sparkled through the stained glass windows on the landing and reflected the gold flecks in Reed's eyes that burned with desire. For her.

She led him down the dimly lit hall toward Nadine's room, her room now. He had never been her sister's lover. But even if he had been, would she have been able to fight feelings this intense?

She doubted it.

"Sasha, if I lie on that bed with you again, I won't be able to stop at kisses," he warned her, his deep voice vibrating with honor and desire.

An irresistible combination.

Chapter Ten

Sasha wasn't about to resist Reed, not anymore.

"The house is empty," she said. "Jerry and Mrs. Arnold have gone into town. Annie and Barbie are outside. With the way the sun's finally shining, I think they'll stay out for a while. Annie's safe, isn't—"

He laid his finger across her lips. "My deputy will be back from lunch by now. He's out there, too. She's fine."

A breath sighed out her relief. "You're right. No one would hurt her. They have no reason to hurt her."

She hadn't inherited anything. Sasha had.

"No one would hurt Annie," he agreed, his gaze intent on Sasha's face. Emotion swirled in the green depths of his eyes. Was he remembering yesterday, seeing her image on the beach, dead?

She shivered, pushing the memory from her mind.

"After what you said to Barbie, I think she'd defend her with her life."

"What did I say?" She couldn't remember, having been distracted by Reed the minute he'd stepped through the door. All she'd been able to think about had been their kisses the day before.

"Be careful."

Maybe she needed to heed her own advice. But she didn't feel like being careful. She felt like being reckless, a little like Nadine. But Nadine was gone.

All she had was Annie now.

"I thought Annie might be yours. I even asked you, but you never said…"

"You hit a sore subject," he admitted. "I wished she was mine."

"You and your wife never had children?" she asked, curious about this woman he'd loved enough to marry. But she braced herself for his reply.

He closed his eyes. "We would have. The baby would have been born about the same time Annie was, if Laurie hadn't aborted her…or him. I never knew. She didn't tell me that. She didn't tell me about the abortion until it was all over."

He laughed, the hollow sound vibrating with bitterness. "She didn't tell me a lot until it was too late."

The pain he'd suffered made Sasha's wedding-day embarrassment insignificant. No. He wouldn't trust again, not after what his ex-wife had put him through.

And she couldn't blame him. But as she'd already admitted, she couldn't resist him, either.

"I'm sorry, Reed." And she would be, after she risked her heart only to have it broken again. "But I'm not Laurie."

"What are you saying?"

"This," she said, reaching up to wind her arms around his neck. Then she grazed his lips with teasing kisses.

He swung her up, kicking the door shut before striding toward the bed. "Kisses aren't going to be enough, Sasha, not nearly enough..."

She reached between them, attacking the buttons on his shirt, tugging it from his shoulders. Now that she'd conquered her fears, power coursed through her, filling her with heady excitement.

Freedom.

And desire like she'd never tasted.

"I want it all," she demanded, moving her lips down his throat where his pulse beat madly. Then she pressed kisses across his chest, the muscles rippling beneath her lips. "I want you, Reed."

His hands, not quite steady, cupped her face, lifting her chin so that their gazes met and held. "And I want *you,* Sasha. Only you."

His words were more moving than any endearment, any declaration. She blinked hard, fighting the threat of tears from her eyes.

But it was harder to fight the love creeping into her heart. She could make love with him, but she couldn't let herself *love* him. That would only lead to heartache, and she'd already had her fill of that.

Her breath shuddered out as her pulse raced. "Reed..." She wouldn't say anymore. To protect herself, she had to hold in the words. But she couldn't hold in the feelings anymore. She reached up, threading her fingers through his hair to guide his mouth to hers. She kissed him with the passion he'd reawakened in her and more…more desire than she'd ever felt for her ex-fiancé.

He groaned. "Sasha, it's been a long time for me."

A smile teased her lips, and she found herself teasing him. "I'll be gentle."

He laughed, then kissed her hard. "I can't promise that I'll be."

"I'm not asking for any promises," she said.

Given their pasts, their present, it was how it had to be. No promises.

His green eyes darkened, and a furrow formed in his brow. But he didn't argue. Instead he kissed her again, sipping at her lips, sliding his tongue along the curve of her bottom one.

She opened for him, welcoming him inside. But she wanted more.

"You're right," she moaned. "Kisses aren't enough." She reached for his belt buckle, but he caught her hand.

"You first," he said, straddling her and easing back on his haunches. "Take off your clothes, Sasha."

Sadness and guilt pulled at her. The jeans and sweater weren't hers. They were Nadine's. But Reed had never been. Her heart lifted a little.

She sat up, then rose to her knees. They were close on the bed, heat radiated from his bare chest. She resisted the urge to nuzzle the soft dark hair covering his muscles. Instead she pulled the sweater up and off.

Then she tossed her head to knock her hair from her eyes, sending it swirling around her bare shoulders.

He gasped. "You're so damned beautiful. I've never seen anyone as beautiful."

She opened her mouth to scoff at his lie, but then she caught his gaze, the intensity and honesty in it. He wasn't lying. And she'd never felt more beautiful.

She reached for the clasp of her bra, purposefully thrusting her breasts against the lacy cups as she arched her back.

Another groan tore from his throat. And his big hands settled on her shoulders, sliding the straps down her arms. Then the bra slid down, too, the cups falling away from her breasts.

"So damned beautiful," he said again. "I couldn't sleep last night, couldn't do anything but think of you... like this."

"Me, too," she admitted. "I want you so much."

She slid her arms around his shoulders, crushing her breasts against his chest. His hair teased the sensitive peaks, and she arched, aching for more, aching for all he could give her.

He moved his hips, and she felt the hard ridge of his erection straining against his jeans. "I want you, Sasha."

Easing her hand between them, she fumbled with his belt buckle again. "Then take me..."

And he did. First he took her mouth in another bone-melting kiss. His tongue stroked in and out, teasing her with what he intended to do to her body. Then he took her breasts, first with his hands, cupping, molding, running his thumbs over the hard nipples.

Heat pooled between her legs as her stomach quivered. His tongue moved down, over those sensitive points. Stroking, suckling…

Coherent thought left her mind, and she stroked her hands along his muscled back, down the bulging biceps of his arms, down the arrow of hair toward the belt buckle she'd finally undone.

Metal rasped as she pulled the zipper down. The sound echoed as he pulled down hers. Then he tugged off her jeans, taking the wisp of lace panties with them. His hands, big and hard, stroked over her naked buttocks, molding them before sliding down in sweeping caresses over her thighs. She parted them for him, for the erection springing free of the jeans he kicked off.

He stroked a finger through the dark tangle of curls at the apex of her thighs. She writhed against the sheets as he slid one, then two fingers between her folds. Biting her lip, she tried to hold in the cry, but it burst free as she shuddered against his hand. "Reed, I need you…"

"Kill me," he groaned. "Just kill me. I don't have any protection. We can't—we shouldn't…"

But she'd reached down, her hand encircling his glistening flesh. "Reed…"

Then she remembered what she'd found on an earlier search of her sister's room. She turned her head toward the bedside table. "Open the drawer, there's a box…"

He reached across her, finding the condoms Nadine

had kept beside her bed. His hands shook as he donned one. "Sasha…"

She lifted her legs, wrapping them around his waist as he eased inside her. And eased some more. He was so damned big, so hard, so strong…so hot.

When he moved, she cried out as her body convulsed around him. And he kept moving, stroking in and out. She held on, as wave after wave of pleasure crashed over her. "Reed, Reed!"

He stiffened in her arms, crying out her name as he found his release. "Sasha, Sasha…"

"SASHA…"

Sasha tried to ignore the voice as she moved her cheek against Reed's bare chest. They'd fallen asleep, her name on his lips.

But he wasn't calling her now.

"Sasha…"

A ghost called her.

She hadn't heard *her* last night. She'd thought that after finding her body, that after seeing her dead, she would stop hearing her.

"Sasha…"

But that was Nadine.

Nadine calling her name.

Why? Why could she hear her now? She knew she was dead. She'd seen her corpse, her eyes open in death, her throat slashed….

The voice grew fainter, sounding as if she stood outside the room, in the hall. She kept calling.

It wasn't a dream. Sasha wasn't sleeping. She could feel the heat of Reed's body, clasped so tightly to hers. Naked skin sliding against naked skin. She didn't want to leave his arms. But the voice kept calling…

She couldn't wake him, couldn't admit her craziness to him. Not again. Slowly she eased from his arms, crawling out of the tangled sheets.

Despite the urgency of the whisper, modesty stopped her from walking out the door naked. She tugged on her discarded jeans and sweater, then glanced at Reed before she followed the beckoning voice. His muscular chest rose and fell with each breath as he slept deeply, undisturbed by either her absence or Nadine's whisper.

He couldn't hear her.

Only Sasha could.

Her heartbeat increased with the volume of the whisper. Maybe she was losing her mind, but she wasn't concerned about that. She was concerned about whatever had compelled Nadine to reach out to her again….

Annie.

Breath catching in her lungs, she hurried down the hall toward the nursery. It was the little girl's nap time. The nanny should have tucked her into her crib with the blanket Reed had given her.

But the crib was empty, the room quiet. Not even the rocker moved in the stillness of the nursery.

Then Nadine called out again, her husky whisper full of fear and horror. "Sasha…"

"Tell me, Nadine. Tell me where she is," Sasha implored the empty space. She couldn't see her sister, not now.

Only on the beach yesterday.

She hadn't seen anything to indicate that that voice wasn't only in her head. Wasn't just a figment of her imagination and a product of her all-consuming guilt.

She shouldn't have let the nanny take Annie off alone. *She* should have taken her for a walk. Instead she'd been making love with Reed....

She took a deep breath, forcing down the rising hysteria. *Think, Sasha.*

Annie was fine. She was probably just in another part of the house. With that thought in mind, Sasha searched...going into rooms she'd never been in before, each one as exquisitely decorated as the next...and empty.

The kitchen.

The walk and the fresh air would have made them hungry. They were probably downstairs, getting a snack before dinner. Sasha rushed toward the steps, her feet hardly touching them as she descended in haste. She ran across the dining room and pushed open the door to the kitchen.

A knife clattered to the counter as Mrs. Arnold jumped at the intrusion. "Oh, my God," she said, clutching her chest. "What's the matter with you?"

"Have you seen Annie?"

The older woman picked up the knife again, her fingers trembling against the wooden handle as she sliced the long blade through a peeled potato. "She's with Barbie."

"You've seen them?"

"No. If the child's not with you, she's with the nanny. That was the way it was with your sister. In some ways you're like her." Distaste twisted the older woman's lips.

She must have guessed where Sasha had been…and with whom. "So you haven't seen them?"

"I just told you—"

"What about Jerry?"

"I don't know. He helped me carry the groceries from the ferry, then he went out to the gardens. You'd have to ask him. What's wrong? It's a beautiful spring day. I'm sure they're outside enjoying it."

Instead of being inside, in a darkened bedroom.

"I don't know," she admitted. "But they've been gone a while. Annie would be tired."

And a ghost had called her name.

"She's fine," Mrs. Arnold assured her. "Barbie has a big mouth, but her heart is just as big. She loves that child. She'd never hurt her."

But what about Nadine?

Had the resentful nanny hurt her? Had Mrs. Arnold? Sasha had to suspect them all. She couldn't trust any of them. Maybe not even herself.

She headed back upstairs, listening for the whisper. Sunlight spilled from the nursery across the hall carpet. She turned toward it, drawn to the light. But the nursery was just as empty, just as quiet as before.

"Where are you, Nadine?"

Before, she had dreaded it. Now she wanted to hear the voice again, sought it out for guidance.

"Sasha…"

But it wasn't Nadine calling her name.

A DRAFT OF COLD AIR whispered across his skin, waking Reed from a sweet dream. But dreaming of Sasha was nothing like the reality, the fire and passion of the flesh-and-blood woman. His heart rate quickened, his breath coming faster and shallower at just the thought of her.

But he awoke alone, his reaching arms finding only empty air. "Sasha…"

Where had she gone? Had regret pulled her from his arms? He should be feeling some himself. He had a murder to solve, but instead of finding a friend's killer, he was making love to her sister, her twin.

Damn. It had been making *love*. His heart softened with it, but it was too damaged, too bitter to ease open and let her in. He couldn't risk it again. And maybe that was his greatest regret.

He glanced at his watch, groaning at the two hours he'd stolen from the day. He didn't have time for this now. He had to make some more calls, check some more leads….

But first he had to find Sasha and make sure she was all right. "Sasha…"

And when he found her, sitting in the rocking chair in the empty nursery, he saw that she wasn't all right. Bathed in sunshine, she looked celestial, like a beautiful black-haired angel. But her face was pale, her blue gaze troubled as she met his.

"Sasha," he called out again. "What's wrong?" he asked, his heart aching at the sight of her anxiety.

Had what they'd done caused her this much distress?

"I don't know," she said, her voice breaking with emotion. "I have a strange feeling. Annie's still out with the nanny, and—"

"It's not raining for once," he said, squinting against the sunshine flooding the room. "I'm sure they're still outside playing."

She shook her head. "I can't explain it. But I *know* we've got to find them."

"Where have you looked?" he asked, because he was sure she had.

"The house. Mrs. Arnold hasn't seen them."

"They were outside. We'll check the grounds." He didn't tell her exactly how much area the grounds encompassed. The estate had the most acreage on the island, some of it heavily wooded. He knew because he'd searched every inch of it for Annie's mother's body. Now he would search for Annie. Some of Sasha's anxiety touched him, reaching deep inside and spurring his fear for the child's safety.

He did another cursory check of the house to see if they'd come inside while Sasha had been in the nursery. But Mrs. Arnold still hadn't seen them. Confusion knitted her forehead over their urgency. She didn't understand.

He didn't entirely, either, but he needed to reassure Sasha. And the only way he could do that would be to put her niece into her arms, safe and sound.

After Mrs. Arnold's short response, Sasha headed toward the door. He followed, grabbing her coat from the hook at the back door. Even though the sun shone, the day had slipped into late afternoon, and a cool breeze would be blowing off the lake.

He caught her on the porch, draping the jacket over her shoulders. When he lifted her hair from under the collar, his hands brushing against her neck, she shivered. His gut tightened with desire, but her contagious anxiety pushed it aside.

For now.

Until they found Annie. And they would. And she'd be safe. *She had to be.*

Boots shuffled across the porch toward him. Reed turned toward his young deputy.

"Sir," Tommy greeted him with respect even though a little smirk played around his mouth and a flush stained his cheekbones. Did everyone on the island know what he and Sasha had been doing?

"Tommy," Reed said. "Have you seen Barbie and the little girl?"

The kid's face flushed more, betraying his crush on the young nanny. "When you came, I left for lunch, like you said. I didn't see them in town."

"How long were you gone?"

"Carol rushed my order, but the inn was pretty busy. Half hour. Maybe forty-five minutes." The young man was too literal to exaggerate, so Reed trusted his reply.

"And you haven't seen them since you got back?"

He shook his head. "No. Just saw Mrs. Arnold and Jerry come back from town. Nobody else."

Reed sighed.

"Is there a problem, Sheriff?"

He'd like to brush off his concern and Sasha's. But he couldn't lie to her. "There might be. I need your help searching for them. Talk to Mr. Scott in the carriage house. Maybe they stopped there to visit."

"What can we do?" Sasha asked, speaking for the first time since he'd found her in the nursery. Her face still held no trace of color, only wide-eyed fear.

"We'll search the grounds."

But the path through the gardens revealed no trace of the nanny and the child. They found the old gardener kneeling in a flower bed. As they approached, Sasha reached for Reed's hand, her nails digging into his skin. Was she scared of the old man? Why?

"Jerry," Reed said, startling the gardener. Dirt sprayed into the air from the trowel he lifted with a jerk of his gnarled hand.

"Sheriff." His squinty-eyed gaze moved over Sasha. "Miss Michaelson."

Sasha nodded, her thick hair tumbling into her face. "Have you seen my niece?" she asked the old man, her voice holding a slight quaver.

Reed suddenly wondered how these people had been treating Sasha to warrant such uneasiness. Why had he left her alone with them? He cursed his lack of sensitivity.

"No, miss," he said, his expression intent on her face. Other people stared at her, no doubt seeing a resemblance to Nadine.

Until yesterday, when Reed had seen Nadine's body on the beach, he'd forgotten about it. When he looked at her, he saw only Sasha, not Nadine.

Jerry continued, "The old woman and I came back from town just a while ago. I saw only the deputy at the door. No one else."

"Mr. Scott?" Reed asked.

"No, sir. Only the kid, I mean, deputy."

Reed thought of Tommy as a kid, too. He'd seen things he hoped to hell the kid never did. But Sasha already had…when she'd found her sister's body on the beach yesterday.

They searched the grounds around the house. Next would be the woods and the beach. He turned toward Sasha. "Why don't you go back inside? The wind's picking up. Tommy and I will search—"

She dropped his hand—he thought to comply with his suggestion. Instead she lifted her chin, her eyes full of anger and resolve.

"I'm helping you search." Her usually soft voice hardened, brooking no argument from him.

"I'm going to the beach next, Sasha," he warned her.

Sasha swayed as if he'd spun her in a dizzying circle, like Annie loved for him to do. Then the child would walk around like a drunken sailor, giggling her curly little head off.

"Just stay here," he advised, hoping for both their sakes that she would listen. He wanted to calm her fears, not add to them. "I'll be right back."

He headed toward the path leading down to the

beach. A piece of yellow crime-scene tape lay in the grass next to the trail. Someone had ripped it off the two stakes flanking the path.

Why the hell would the nanny take the little girl to the place where her mother's dead body had washed ashore? He hoped he was wrong. He hoped it was some kids from town, driven by curiosity to break the law.

Closer to the beach he found a small pink tennis shoe. Had she lost it on the trail, or had it dropped from her foot as someone carried her down the steep slope?

Heart racing, he left the shoe, not wanting to disturb any possible evidence. His gut churned as he forced himself to respond as a lawman and not the father he wished he could have been for the little girl. Then he turned his attention toward the rocky shore. "Annie!"

The waves raced toward the rocks, the roar of the rushing water muffling his voice and Sasha's approach until she grasped his arm with one hand. The little shoe was in her other shaking hand.

"Oh, my God, she's down here. Where? Where is she?" Her voice shook, too.

"We'll find them," he said, but he didn't add a promise, just a silent prayer.

Their shoes slipped on the slick rocks as they scrambled along the shore, away from the path. She lost her footing, and he grabbed at her arm, keeping her from falling where she might have struck her head on the craggy beach.

He wanted to send her to the house again, but he knew she wouldn't go back, not without Annie. So he moved his hand from her arm, wrapping it around her small waist, holding her close against him.

As they neared the area where she'd found Nadine, he studied her pale face. Her body trembled against his as she leaned on him. As well as physical support, he wanted to offer emotional support. He wanted to erase the horrific image from her mind.

She screamed, gesturing behind him.

Breath leaving his lungs, he turned to the taped-off area where Sasha had found Nadine's body. And he found another corpse.

The young nanny stared at them, eyes gaping open in death as her blood bathed the rocks, draining from the gaping wound in her neck.

Chapter Eleven

"Annie!" Sasha screamed, throat burning as desperation clawed at her.

She couldn't think about what might have happened to the child, not while the nanny lay there… murdered. She had to believe her niece was all right. She had to believe it, or she'd lose what was left of her mind.

Tears burned her eyes, but she blinked them back, concentrating on calling the child's name and praying that she would answer. "Annie!"

Sasha tore away from Reed's strong arms, feet sliding across the rocks as she ran farther down the shore. Nadine had trusted her child to Sasha's care. How badly had she let her sister down?

How could she have let the child out of her sight when there was a killer on the loose?

Nadine's killer.

She glanced back over her shoulder, at Barbie's dead body. And the killer had killed again.

Just once?

Her heart raced, and she could hardly catch her breath as she screamed, "Annie!"

But the wind and crash of the waves whipped away the sound of her voice. Despite her efforts, she could barely hear herself.

She would keep looking, keep calling…

"Annie!"

She scrambled around a boulder, breath catching in her lungs as she found the little girl.

Annie sat on the rocks, pant legs wet from the encroaching waves. She played with some small pebbles, piling them up as she constructed walls of a structure for which only she knew the purpose. To keep her safe, to protect her from harm?

That was Sasha's job. And she'd failed…miserably. What if the killer had hurt the child? What if Annie had waded into the cold lake, the waves crashing over her?

"Annie," she said again, throat clogged with tears. "Annie."

The little girl cocked her head toward her aunt, her bright eyes dulled with sleepiness. "Mommy," she said before turning back toward her pebble piles.

Sasha rushed forward, lifting the child into her arms, holding her tight against her chest.

"I'm sorry, I'm so sorry," she murmured into Annie's tousled curls, damp from the spray of the foaming waves. "I promise I won't let anything happen to you, baby. I'll keep you safe."

From now on.

She'd nearly lost the child to a murderer and the lake. How could she have been so irresponsible?

When they were growing up, that had always been Nadine; *she'd* been the reckless one. Sasha had always played it safe, not that it had saved her from getting hurt, but she'd never been as careless as she'd been since arriving on Sunset Island.

Maybe Nadine had made a mistake in leaving her little girl to Sasha. Maybe she would have been safer with someone else, with Reed. Sasha pulled Annie closer, pressing her tight to her heart. She didn't want to lose her, even though she didn't deserve her.

The cold wind whipped around them, the little girl's shiver setting off one in Sasha. Then warmth enveloped her as Reed wrapped his arms around them both, his shaking hand tousling the little girl's curls.

"There she is, there's our beautiful girl," he said, voice gruff with emotion.

Our. Not his. Not hers.

But she couldn't read anything into his words. He was just relieved the little girl was safe, especially since another young woman was not.

Sasha tipped her head back, meeting his gaze, knowing the tears brightening his eyes were falling from hers. Tears of relief, tears of anguish.

Another woman had been murdered as violently as Nadine. Had Annie been down by the water when the murder occurred? Sasha doubted that Barbie would have been that uncaring of the child's safety. She would have kept Annie close. Close enough to witness her nanny's murder?

What had the little girl seen?

SASHA LEANED against the nursery doorway, captivated by the image before her. Reed knelt beside the crib, stroking his big hand over Annie's small face. She hated to disturb him, but she had to know. "Is she all right?"

He nodded, his shoulders barely moving. She knew he carried the same amount of guilt she did. Given his job, maybe more. She shouldn't have trusted the nanny, shouldn't have let her take Annie off alone.

And why had she? So she could selfishly act on her feelings for Reed. Feelings she should have continued to resist because they could lead to nothing but more heartache.

How much more heartache would Annie have to suffer? She'd lost the two people closest to her. And she might have witnessed the murder of one of them.

She voiced her fear, "Do you think she saw what happened to Barbie?"

He shook his head. "No. I doubt it. She talked about the water, the stones, nothing else."

"Why would Barbie take her *there?*" she asked, voice cracking with the emotions swirling through her. "Morbid curiosity?"

He stood up and turned toward her, shuttering his expression. What was he trying to keep from her? "Sasha, you don't need to worry about—"

Because Annie was asleep, she held in an outraged

shout…barely. "How dare you? I lost my sister already. Today I almost lost my niece. I need to do more than worry. I need to know what's going on…" *Before she left.*

After what had happened today, after the danger Annie had been in, Sasha had no choice. In order to keep Nadine's daughter safe, she had to leave Sunset Island.

Reed joined her in the doorway, so tall and strong. But she couldn't count on him for protection. She'd learned five years ago that she couldn't count on anyone.

His hand cupped her elbow, steering her into the hall. "This is a police investigation—"

She cast another glance toward the sleeping child. "This affects me." And Annie. "I deserve to know."

A ragged sigh slipped through his lips. "Okay, you're right."

So she asked again, "Why did she take Annie down to the beach?"

"Sasha, remember that I have no hard evidence. Yet." His green eyes gleamed with determination and something even fiercer, anger. He took it personally that someone was killing people for whose safety he considered himself responsible.

"This is just supposition," he cautioned.

"Let me hear your supposition." Because she had a feeling that his instincts were probably much more reliable than hers.

"Barbie was probably meeting someone," he said.

"Who?"

"Apparently your sister's killer."

Her killer. Poor Barbie. "So this is the same person? A serial killer?"

She shuddered. The island seemed so peaceful, so quaint. But she knew its isolation, its eeriness.

"That was my first thought." Dread deepened his voice. "But I think it's more involved than that."

More personal. "She knew who killed Nadine."

"I think so."

And he'd interrogated the girl but gotten nothing out of her. Sasha hadn't guessed the extent of the guilt he felt, but she felt it now, as if she were close enough to share his burden. But they weren't close. Despite how intimate they'd been that afternoon, they were relative strangers.

Weren't they?

She reached out, running her fingertips along his jaw, hoping to soothe his troubled soul. "You're not to blame for any of this. Only one person is."

The killer.

He caught her hand, bringing it toward his mouth for a quick kiss. "I may not be to blame, but I'm just as at fault. It's my responsibility to protect these people. I failed." His breath shuddered out. "I failed your sister, Sasha. And today I failed Annie…and Barbie."

"She knew who the killer was. She should have told you. She could have saved herself." But she'd been young and resentful. "Was she part of it? Part of Nadine's murder?"

Maybe it hadn't been coincidence that she'd taken Annie for a walk *that day,* too. Maybe it had been part of the plot to kill Nadine.

"I don't know. I searched her room. Again. I had searched the entire house after Nadine's death, but I hadn't found this then." He withdrew a folded piece of paper from his jeans pocket. "It's addressed to you. Nadine wrote it."

She'd already heard from Nadine once that day. If she hadn't, if Nadine's frantic whisper hadn't wakened her, Annie might have been carried away on those encroaching waves. She might have been lost in the lake just as her mother's body had been for too many days....

"Nadine," she said, her breath catching.

God, her feelings for her twin were so complicated. If only...

Reed squeezed her shoulder, the grasp of his big hand offering little comfort as it reminded her of that afternoon, of those stolen hours of passionate kisses and hot caresses...and so much more than she'd ever thought possible.

"It's not the whole letter," he said.

She pulled herself from her wanton thoughts and reawakened desires. "You kept some of it?" she asked.

He shook his head, frustration tightening the hard line of his jaw. "No, someone else did."

The killer.

"Like Barbie, Nadine knew the killer, too," she guessed, "even before he'd killed. He must have been threatening her." As Reed had suspected, when Nadine's money ran out, the killer had gotten rid of her. "Why not tell you?"

Why not tell *her?* Regret squeezed like a cold hand around Sasha's heart. Because she had told Nadine that she never wanted to hear from her again. Ever. For any reason. They were no longer sisters.

But if she hadn't felt like she could come to Sasha, why not Reed? Had she been involved in something illegal? Something she'd paid a blackmailer to keep secret? "Why hadn't she asked *someone* for help?"

Tears stung Sasha's eyes. *Damn her.* If only Nadine had reached out, she would be alive…not a ghost in an eerie old house. But maybe that was why she'd called Charles, for help. But it had already been too late. But then, maybe Charles had been more destroyer than savior. Obviously, Sasha had never known what the man was capable of.

Reed pressed the letter into her hand. "You need to read it."

She didn't want to. No one had ever hurt her as much as Nadine had, not even Charles. Her fingers trembled against the paper. "Don't you need to keep it? Isn't it evidence?"

"Yes," he admitted.

She tried to hand it back, but he fisted his hands. "I'm bending the rules because you need to read it, Sasha. Then you can give it back to me."

"I'm leaving tomorrow," she said, the words coming out in a rush before she could change her mind.

No surprise flickered in his green eyes. He'd known and he wasn't going to ask her to stay. Maybe that was why he was so adamant that she read the words her sister had written for her.

So that when she left, she'd have a better understanding of her sister. For her sake? Or Nadine's?

She stopped fighting to hand the letter back, instead she curled her fingers around the rumpled paper. Perhaps Nadine had written it and then wadded it up to throw it away before mailing it. Maybe Barbie had found it in her employer's trash. Why hadn't Nadine sent it?

The angry words she'd hurled at her sister when Nadine had called her after the wedding that had never taken place resounded in Sasha's head. *I never want to hear from you again. You're dead to me.* And now she was.

She blinked back tears. "Okay. I'll read it."

He squeezed her hand, then released it and walked away. She wanted to ask him so many things. About the letter.

And about them. Did he care that she was leaving? Would she see him again before she did?

She didn't ask. And although she didn't hear her this time, she could almost *feel* Nadine calling her back into the nursery. Drawn to the rocker, she settled into it and unfolded the letter.

Dear Sasha,

I've written you so many times over these past few years, but I've always lost the nerve to send the letter. Maybe this time will be different. I have so much to tell you. I have a daughter. She's so beautiful. So smart. So good. She's definitely more like you than me. And I think often that she should have been yours.

Sasha sucked in a quick breath. Did that mean—was Charles Annie's father? If he realized, he could take her away, and he might very well be the one who'd killed Annie's mother.

She read on.

You would make a much better mother than I will ever be. But I'm all she has. Well, me and this wonderful man I've met here on the island. Nothing's happened between us. Like Annie, I've often thought he would be better off with you. He's been hurt so damned bad that he's not likely to ever take a chance again. I worry that you feel the same way. That I've hurt you so badly that you'll never take a chance on me again. And so, like my other letters, I'll probably never mail this one. But please know, I am so, so sorry for being self-ish and hurtful to you. You never did anything to deserve it. You just loved me. And I've never de-served love.

I've tried to contact Mom and Dad, too. Be-coming a parent has made me understand them. Finally. But their number is disconnected and they have no new listing. I hope they're healthy and happy. That they're not working too hard. They deserve an easier life than they had, than I ever gave them. Thank God for you, Sasha.

If anything happens to me, I want you to raise Annie. I know she'll be safe with you. And I know that even though I killed whatever love you had for me, you will love her. I'm sorry about Charles. For what it's worth, I truly loved him. Probably still do. But I've made so many mistakes…

And the letter stopped there, at the end of the second page. Where was the third? Despite what he'd said, had Reed kept it for evidence?

Or had Nadine's killer kept it because Nadine had disclosed his identity?

Had she confessed her sins and, in doing so, implicated this person? Is that why she'd died? Because she'd been about to make amends for all her misdeeds?

Sasha set the chair into motion, tears falling onto the pages in her lap. "Oh, Nadine, you're wrong. You didn't kill my love for you. I love you still…."

SHE WAS LEAVING. Reed couldn't blame her. He couldn't ask her to stay. For her safety, for Annie's, it was better that Sasha leave Sunset Island. But watching her leave, taking Annie with her, would eat away at what was left of his soul.

The bedroom door opened. She stopped and gasped, hand pressed to her heart. "I thought you left."

She might have preferred that. He couldn't tell from

her expression, and she refused to meet his eyes, hers red with the tears she must have cried over Nadine's letter. Maybe he shouldn't have left her alone to read it. But she always fought so hard to hold in her tears if someone was around. And he'd felt that she needed to weep for Nadine. Maybe her tears would wash away her guilt.

"I didn't leave." He stated the obvious but only to reassure her. "I'm staying tonight."

Tomorrow it wouldn't be necessary. Tomorrow she would be gone.

"For Annie's protection?" she asked, indicating the baby monitor she held in one hand while the other clutched her sister's letter.

"That's part of it," he admitted, flinching as he remembered the sight of the little girl sitting alone on the beach, the waves sucking at her pant legs, about to drag her away from him. He wasn't any better at protecting Annie than he'd been at protecting her mother. No, it would be safest for Sasha and Annie to leave Sunset Island.

"And the other part?" she asked, setting the monitor on the bedside table.

"You."

"Here's your *evidence*," she said, extending the paper toward him, parts of it transparent from the tears she'd shed upon it. "Do you have the third page?"

His jaw cracked as he clenched it, his anger at the killer, not at her obvious lack of trust in what he'd already told her. She didn't really believe that he was keeping information from her. "No."

She nodded. "So the killer has the rest of my sister's letter. Is that why Barbie was killed? She was blackmailing whoever did this to Nadine?"

Just as he believed whoever had killed Nadine had been blackmailing her. Ironic that the blackmailer had been blackmailed himself.

"I'll find her killer," he promised her again. He might have left some cases unsolved in Detroit, when no leads and no suspects had led to arrests. But he wouldn't let this case get cold. Nadine deserved justice.

"I believe you," she said.

Not *trust* you. Did she trust anyone after what Nadine and Charles had done to her, how badly they'd hurt her?

"About this afternoon," he began.

She flinched, and he glimpsed the guilt in her blue eyes. She hadn't cried enough tears to wash it all away.

Her voice quavered as she said, "It was a mistake. I know that. I never would have forgiven myself if we hadn't found Annie in time."

Neither would he have. "But we did."

She expelled a shaky breath. "Thank God we did."

Curiosity nagged at him, and he asked, "How did you know she was in danger? You were so certain that she was."

She shrugged her slender shoulders as her cheeks flushed with faint pink color. "You wouldn't believe me if I told you."

"Try me."

A sigh slipped through her lips. "It sounds too crazy, makes me sound too crazy."

Crazy. He understood that. Thinking of her leaving tomorrow was making him crazy.

He swallowed hard, then spoke, "What I wanted to say about this afternoon was that, although I regretted the timing, I didn't regret anything else."

She tilted her face toward him, her blue eyes soft and vulnerable. "You didn't?"

"No," Reed said, stepping closer to her. "It meant a lot to me."

Too much.

His heart beat harder at her closeness, hammering in his chest as feelings crashed over him. Too many feelings. One he didn't dare name because, after his divorce, he'd vowed to never feel it again.

She nodded. "Me, too."

Then she pushed a hand through her tousled black hair. "And maybe that's crazier than..."

"Than what?"

"Never mind. It doesn't matter."

Even if she stayed, he had nothing to offer her. Nothing but one more night.

"It matters. You matter. I hate to see you leave," he confessed.

A smile touched her lips. "I can't say I'll miss the island."

Just like his ex.

She added, "Maybe if the circumstances had been different..."

If they'd been different people, with different pasts, different presents…

"I'm going to sleep in the nursery tonight," she said. "I just came back in here to pack."

But she didn't move toward the closet. Instead she moved toward him, sliding her arms around his neck. "But I will miss you, Reed."

Her fingers on his nape pulled his head down till his lips met hers. He tasted salt from the tears she'd shed. Alone. He shouldn't have left her alone to read the letter. He wouldn't leave her alone again tonight.

"Sasha…" Her name slipped out of his lips on a groan. He'd never wanted anyone like he wanted her, not even his ex-wife. His hands, shaking with the force of his desire for her, slid up her back, pressing her closer, as he deepened their kiss.

She shuddered and moaned his name, sliding her lips from his. "I should be packing," she said, even as her fingers clutched at his hair.

He cupped her face, searching her eyes for her true feelings. Did she want him to leave her…like this? But he'd never been able to guess at a woman's emotions and had vowed never to trust another one with his.

"What do you want, Sasha?" he asked.

"You, Reed."

For one more night.

She didn't add those words, but they both knew that was all they'd have…because she was leaving. Despite his efforts to protect his heart, he knew it would still hurt when she was gone.

And if he doubted her words, her actions told him how she felt as she tore the buttons on his shirt free and pushed it from his shoulders. "Make love to me, Reed."

His control snapped, and he discarded her clothes just as impatiently until she stood before him, gloriously naked. Then he had to catch his breath as it struggled to escape his lungs in a deep groan. The lamplight cast shadows on her pale skin, on the hollows and the lush curves. Her gorgeous hair lay in a gleaming ebony cloud around her shoulders, stray locks brushing over the tips of her breasts. "You are so beautiful."

Her eyes dilated, the blue becoming just a brilliant rim around the black pupils. "You're not so bad yourself, Sheriff," she said as her gaze skimmed over his bare chest. Then she reached for his belt, unclasping it before pushing down his jeans.

His erection strained against his knit boxers until she pushed those down, too. Then she dropped to her knees, staring up at him as she closed her lips around the tip of him.

"Sasha," he groaned, his fingers tangling in her hair. He intended to lift her up, but the slide of her mouth along his erection weakened his knees. "Sasha…"

This wasn't what he'd intended. He'd wanted to make this a night *she* wouldn't forget…so she wouldn't forget him when she went home. But instead of slow and gentle, she'd unleashed him. Slow and gentle were the last things on his mind or what was left of it.

When she finally slid her lips free, he lifted her and tossed her onto the bed so hard that she nearly bounced.

A flicker of remorse burned in him, but then she giggled. He hadn't heard that since she'd arrived on the island, hadn't seen as carefree a smile as the one that graced her mouth.

"My turn," he growled as he followed her down. His lips touched hers, briefly tasting her smile, before skimming down her throat where her pulse beat madly. For him. For what he was about to do to her. And he intended to do everything to make her writhe and moan.

And never forget him.

He teased one breast with the tip of his tongue, laving circles around the nipple while his fingers played with the hardened tip of her other breast, caressing and caressing as she squirmed beneath him.

"Reed…"

"Do you want this?" he asked, as he touched his tongue to the nipple before suckling it into his mouth.

She bucked on the bed, pressing her hips against him. "Reed…"

He anointed the other breast with wet kisses before trailing his tongue down her navel, dipping in once, twice, before slipping farther down her body.

"Reed…"

He slid his palms along her thighs, so silky against his skin. So creamy. Then he trailed his fingers to the heart of her, driving her up, so that she shuddered and thrashed her head against the pillows.

Feeling her heat, her wetness made him greedy for more, and he replaced his fingers with his mouth, so that he could taste her intimately.

"Reed!" she screamed his name as she came apart in his arms. "Reed!"

He barely had enough control left to don protection before he drove into her. Barely had enough control left to drive her into sobbing ecstasy before he reached his own, shouting out her name as he crashed back to reality in her arms. And still he wanted more, wanted it to never end.

But in the morning she was leaving. He rolled to his side, pulling her tight against him. Tonight she wouldn't slip from his arms unnoticed.

She laid her head on his shoulder, then pressed a kiss against his skin. "Thank you," she said.

He lifted a brow, too exhausted from their lovemaking to understand her gratitude. And as for *that,* he should be thanking her.

"For letting me read the *evidence.*" She blew out a shaky breath. "It's good to know that she loved me."

Reed was afraid it was an emotion he echoed. How could he let Sasha leave?

Chapter Twelve

The phone rang, jolting Sasha from the only real sleep she'd had since Reed had called to tell her that Nadine was dead. She fumbled with the receiver, bringing it to her ear for the monotonous rhythm of the dial tone. But the phone kept ringing.

"Your cell," a deep voice mumbled in her ear. "It's your cell."

She dropped the receiver and found her cell phone. Before hitting the talk button, she settled back against the warmth of Reed's hard body, grateful for his presence. If only he'd been with her when she'd first learned of Nadine's death…less than a week ago.

Had it really been just a week since she'd met him? It felt longer, like always. She'd never connected with anyone on the levels she connected with Reed, not even Charles, and she'd known him for years.

"Hello," she murmured into the phone.

"Sasha, I hope it's not too late. We called your house earlier today and got your message. Then I nearly forgot to call…what with the time change and everything."

"Mom."

Reed pulled her closer, squeezing her shoulder in silent support.

"Where are you, sweetheart? It's gotta be late now in Michigan."

There was so much she needed to tell her parents, but she didn't know where to begin.

"Where are you, Mom?"

"California. It's so beautiful." Her mother sighed, the sound soft and full of happiness. "The weather is perfect, just perfect."

Perfect. Nothing would be perfect for her mother, not once Sasha shared the horrible news. "I have to tell you something, Mom."

But God, she wished she didn't have to. She wished her twin were still alive.

"What's the matter, sweetheart?" Concern replaced the happiness in her mother's soft voice.

"It's Nadine, Mom."

Her mother sucked in a quick breath. "I didn't think you two had talked since after the…well, what's she done to you now?"

Turned her world upside down. But none of that was Nadine's fault. Her killer was to blame. "Mom, I wish I didn't have to tell you this. Nadine's dead."

Tears slid down Sasha's face as she listened to her mother's broken sobs.

Then her father took the phone. "What's happened, Sasha? Your mother's crying."

"Nadine's dead, Dad."

"Oh, my God."

"Tell Mom that she has a granddaughter. Nadine has a beautiful daughter. I'm here with her, with Annie." And Reed. And although every instinct screamed that she shouldn't be, she was glad he was with her, arms wrapped tightly around her. "We're on Sunset Island. Do you know where that is?"

"Yes, of course. We'd always intended to take you girls up there when you were little." His voice, always so deep and steady, cracked with emotion.

Closing her eyes, she could picture him, hair prematurely gray, deep lines bracketing his mouth and the corners of his blue eyes, which had to be filled with shock.

His voice shook as he went on, "But we could never get enough time off work."

Because of their jobs, they'd never been able to travel, as they'd wanted to when they were young. Sasha had been happy when they'd bought the motor home and finally realized their dream. But this, this news, had to be their worst nightmare.

Losing a child…like she'd almost lost Annie the day before.

Her father cleared his throat. "Honey, we'll leave right now. Maybe we can park the motor home somewhere and get a flight back there today."

"But Dad—"

"We have a granddaughter? We really have a granddaughter?" His breath shuddered out. "I can't believe…"

"She's two, Dad. And she's so beautiful." A soft breath sighed through the baby monitor sitting on the bedside table. "So sweet."

"Nadine was a mother?"

"Everyone says she was a good one. And from how healthy and happy Annie is, I know that she was, Dad." Such a good mother that she had returned from the dead to protect her child from the person who had killed her.

But Sasha couldn't share that belief with anyone, not her parents, not Reed. Or they'd all think she'd gone crazy.

"And the father?" he asked, his voice full of a father's grief in the loss of his child.

Sasha didn't know who Annie's father was, but she couldn't tell her dad that. Why hadn't Nadine revealed that in the letter? Then she remembered, *She should have been yours.* Maybe Nadine *had* told her.

"She left her to me, Dad. I'm her legal guardian."

"That's good. You're so good with kids."

With teenagers. She had no clue how she would raise a toddler on her own and keep her job. But she wouldn't give Annie up, not even to her parents. They'd struggled to raise two children already. She didn't want them to struggle anymore. And Nadine had left Annie to her, had trusted her with the child. Sasha wouldn't let her down, not again.

"Your mother will want to see her." He sighed again. "So do I. We'll find a flight to Sunset Island."

"There isn't an airport on the island, Dad. But don't worry about getting here. I'm coming home—" she glanced at the illuminated dial of the clock on Nadine's bedside table "—today."

He released a ragged sigh. "We can probably get a plot for her…for Nadine…in the same cemetery your grandma's in, in Grand Rapids."

"No, Dad." Even with the third page of the letter missing, Sasha knew Nadine would have wanted her ashes spread on Sunset Island. "I'll take care of it."

"Okay, honey…" And then his voice, always so strong and sure, broke again as he dissolved into ragged sobs.

"Oh, Daddy," Sasha said, her heart breaking with her father's over the death of his daughter.

Reed pressed a kiss on the top of her head, his encircling arms holding her tight to his chest. Although she appreciated his presence, he couldn't take away her pain. She was sure that, in the end, he would only add to it.

REED HAD NEVER BEEN so personally involved in a case. Every part of it tore out another piece of his soul. Sasha's tears, as she'd told her parents about Nadine's death, had been torture for him, like someone shooting off his kneecaps. God, he would have preferred the physical pain to listening to her weep and not being able to stop her tears.

And not being able to stop her from leaving. Today. She was packing now. He'd left before she'd awakened again, but he knew that was what she would be doing. Packing Annie's things and what few things of her own she'd brought. Knowing her as well as he'd come to know her in such a short time, he knew she wouldn't take anything of Nadine's...but her daughter.

He would go back to say goodbye. But he couldn't stand there and watch her pack. Instead he sat in the dining room of the inn, his coffee cooling while he brooded into the depths he suspected were about as black as his soul.

"Sheriff," Norder said as he pulled out the chair across from Reed.

"Sure, join me," Reed said, the sarcasm as bitter on his tongue as the cold coffee. But he'd intended to have another go at Norder, anyway, even though he hadn't found anything when he'd searched the man's room yesterday.

"Thank you." The younger man turned over a coffee cup and waved Carol over to fill it. "For the seat and for *cleaning* my room yesterday."

"You offered," Reed reminded him. He wouldn't have had enough to get a search warrant.

"As you learned for yourself, I have nothing to hide," the younger man said with a smirk that Reed itched to wipe off his face.

Carol snorted over Norder's claim, her ears as sharp as ever, as she approached their table.

"There was another murder," she said, like Reed didn't know it. "That poor nanny. And he's still here." Her eyes hardened with suspicion.

Reed held a hand over his still-full cup. "I've got it, Carol."

And Reed hoped to hell that he did, or that he was at least getting close to catching the killer before he killed again. Carol must have believed him because she nodded and walked off with one last glare at the stranger.

"Brrr," Norder said with an exaggerated shudder.

"Yeah, you're not exactly getting a warm reception here. Why do you stay?" Even as he asked it, he knew.

"Sasha."

Reed's gut clenched, and he fisted his hand on the tabletop. "She hasn't exactly given you a warm reception, either."

"Ouch. Direct hit, Sheriff," Norder said, but the smirk grew, twisting the man's lips.

Lips Sasha had once kissed. The thought of that churned Reed's stomach, the bitter coffee threatening to come back up. He fought against the nausea and the jealousy.

"Sasha's not the reason you came to Sunset Island. I wonder if you would have if *she* had called you. You came here because Nadine called you," he reminded the other man.

"Nadine's dead." Despite the man's flip tone, emotion clouded his eyes. "They are *identical* twins."

Reed's temper, already worn thin, snapped, as did his arm, reaching across the table to grab Norder by the neck. "Sasha is no substitute for Nadine. She's…"

Special. Beautiful. Kind-hearted.

Norder swallowed hard. "She's what?"

"None of your damned business. If I didn't suspect you of murder, I'd throw you off the island myself." He forced his fingers to relax, forced himself to drop his hand from the Norder's throat.

"Afraid of a little competition, Sheriff?" he goaded, rubbing his hand over his neck.

God, Reed wanted to slug the man, but he already had an audience of interested diners. "Don't push your luck, Norder. I might just lock you up."

"You have nothing, Sheriff. Nothing to tie me to either of these murders."

But his gut. Was it instinct or jealousy that made him want this man to be guilty?

"You're here." And that was enough evidence for Reed. Too damned bad it wouldn't be enough for a judge.

"And I'm a stranger. You want it to be me, so you don't have to arrest one of *them*." He gestured around the dining room, startling their interested spectators.

No, he didn't want to arrest one of the people he'd sworn to serve and protect…as he had Nadine. But he'd failed Nadine. And she wasn't the only one who'd suffered for it. Annie had. And Sasha. And Barbie had, as well.

And because he couldn't find the killer, he was about to lose Annie and Sasha. So he had to take a risk. "Someone was blackmailing Nadine."

Norder lifted a blond brow. "Really?"

"You sound surprised."

"It's just, that doesn't sound like something Nadine would tolerate. Maybe something she'd do…"

Despite the two years of friendship they'd shared, Reed had never really known Nadine. She was nothing like her twin despite their identical faces. "She drained all the cash from the estate she inherited. She was paying someone."

"And you think that person's the killer?" Norder took a sip of his coffee, his face serious as he obviously considered what Reed had shared with him. "Why kill the cash cow?"

"Because it dried up. She was broke." Just the house and the grounds left. Sasha's suspicions nagged at him. She'd thought her sister's death was about the house.

Norder nodded, then took another sip of his coffee. "Nadine was hardly the type to save money. She never planned for the future." The man's voice vibrated with excitement in the life he'd lived when he'd been with Nadine. "She lived in the moment."

And now she was dead. "That might have been true when you knew Nadine. But that wasn't the Nadine I knew."

"How well did you know her, Sheriff?" Norder asked, his voice thick with jealousy.

Not well enough to keep her alive.

"I'm the one asking questions, Norder. About blackmail." Reed drew on his years of law enforcement experience. If he'd been back in Detroit, he would have had the guy in an interrogation room. He would have been standing over him, fists on the table, threatening.

He'd never had so much at stake before. The safety of a child and a woman he cared about more than he'd thought he would ever let himself care again.

"I don't know anything about blackmail," Norder said with an insulted sniff. "I'm getting my life together. I'll be finishing medical school soon, starting my residency…"

"That kind of education isn't cheap."

The younger man shrugged. "You'd have to ask my parents about the expense."

He would. He needed to verify everything the man told him. "Problem is that Nadine was only here a short while. She's really not done much on the island that anyone could blackmail her for…"

Unless all the rumors were true.

"So that's where I come in," Charles said, lips lifting into a sneer.

"You knew her well."

He sighed. "Yeah, I did."

"You know about her past."

Norder snorted. "Yeah, shoplifting. Passing bad checks. Maybe lifting a credit card number or two. She ran away from home when she was seventeen. She had to survive. So she used her wits."

Reed sat back, his suspicions shaken by the man's vehement defense of his dead lover. "She was no saint."

"She wasn't Sasha, no," Norder said, bitterness flashing across his face. "But she didn't give a damn about what she'd done. She wouldn't have cared who knew it."

"That was before Annie."

The child had changed everything. Was she Norder's? Was that why the man had stuck around? Was he biding his time before making his paternal claim? Maybe he figured he could claim them both, the child and her aunt.

"You're saying someone might have used her past to take away her kid?" Norder remarked with a soft whistle. "Harsh."

"Yeah."

"Why didn't she go to you? If you two were so close, why didn't she ask you for help?"

Norder had listened to his share of gossip, too. And the same jealousy that ate at Reed's gut over Norder's involvement with Sasha was apparent in the tightness of the other man's jaw.

"I wished to God she had." She'd be alive, and he wouldn't have to live with her death on his conscience. He'd known something was wrong. He damned well should have pressed her for more.

"Maybe she thought you wouldn't understand, being a lawman and all. Everything's so black-and-white for you."

Colors meant nothing to Reed. All he cared about right now were life and death. Sasha's life and Nadine's death.

"Some shoplifting, bad checks?" Reed wouldn't have considered her past enough to make her an unfit parent.

Unless there was more...unless as Sasha suspected,

it wasn't about Nadine's past at all. It was about the house.

"So you really don't have a motive for her death," the man needled.

"Oh, I wouldn't say that. There's always a motive with old lovers." Like Charles's reason for hanging around because Sasha was still on the island.

"But you have to remember this, Sheriff, when you consider motive." The man's eyes gleamed with deep emotion. "I loved Nadine."

"And Sasha?"

"I think *you* love her."

SASHA'S HANDS SHOOK as she folded Annie's tiny clothes into the suitcase she'd found in Nadine's closet. She kept glancing toward the rocking chair, but it didn't move. No one whispered her name.

Why did she miss it?

She hated leaving, but for Annie's safety, she had no choice.

"Want help?" Mrs. Arnold asked from the doorway.

Her offer shouldn't have surprised Sasha. She knew how much the woman wanted her gone. "Not now, but I'll need a hand bringing this stuff down to the ferry."

Would the gnarled gardener be able to carry any of the bags? She doubted it. But Mrs. Arnold was strong, probably strong enough to slash a young woman's throat. She shivered and cast a nervous glance to where Annie played on the floor, humming as she stacked blocks into leaning towers.

"The sheriff planted an officer outside the door again," the woman said, unwittingly relieving some of Sasha's uneasiness at being alone with her.

"Tommy?" she asked.

"Someone a little older, I think," the woman said with a rueful smile. "He'll be able to handle these things. Are you taking it all?"

Sasha shook her head. "No."

As certain as she was that she had to leave to protect Annie, she also knew she wanted to come back...after the killer was caught and it was finally safe.

"What are you going to do about the house?" The older woman was obsessed with the house, not even mentioning what she was sure to know. There was no money for her next month's salary.

Sasha had to talk to the lawyer, had to see how much the expenses were, had to see what she could afford.

Mrs. Arnold's tentative smile faded. "You're going to keep it even though it wasn't rightfully *hers*."

Sasha's chin came up as she came to her sister's defense. "I talked to Mr. Scott. He doesn't believe that."

"He's an artist. He's irresponsible and flighty," Mrs. Arnold said, her tone dismissive as well as disgusted.

"So she wouldn't have left him the house," Sasha said.

And Sasha could keep it, could return to Sunset Island once the killer was caught. She could explore all these feelings she had for Reed and see if he returned any of them.

And her parents might like the house. They'd never owned one, and they deserved easier lives than the ones they'd lived. They deserved a secure future. And if they couldn't afford to keep it, they could sell it and use the proceeds for their retirement. Or she could put it in trust for Annie, so that Annie would have something from her mother.

Mrs. Arnold pursed her lips as if about to speak, then she turned and headed back into the hall.

Sasha's relief that she'd been spared another diatribe about her twin's misdeeds was short-lived.

The woman spoke again, "Mrs. Scott wouldn't have left it to your sister. She had granddaughters of her own. She would have left it for them."

Surprise jolted Sasha, and she paused while putting toys in a case. "What? Mr. Scott had been married?"

"No. But he has two daughters. His mother knew that. She would have left it to them. Not Nadine." Perhaps ashamed that she had shared family secrets, the housekeeper disappeared into the hall again. After a breath-holding moment, Sasha heard her footsteps on the stairs.

The memory of the letter burned in Sasha's mind. Nadine had admitted to many mistakes. Had she swindled the old woman out of her estate? Had she killed her as Mrs. Arnold suspected?

She glanced toward where her niece played in the turret room Nadine had decorated so gaily for her. "What did your mother do?" she asked her.

Annie looked up. "Mommy, come pway."

"I can't, sweetheart. I have to speak to someone." From her sweater pocket, she withdrew her cell phone to call the lawyer. She had put off making her decision long enough. And there were truths she needed to know.

After what had happened yesterday, Barbie's murder, almost losing Annie…she'd put it off too long.

SASHA RAPPED THE KNUCKLES of one hand on the bright-yellow door of the carriage house while she held tight to Annie's hand with the other. When no one answered, she turned to leave, figuring Mr. Scott must have gone to town.

"Wait!" a voice called from above, and she tipped her head back to find the older man hanging half out of a second-story window. "The door's unlocked. Please come up. I have something I want to show you."

She hesitated before reaching for the door handle. She'd already seen enough on the island to give her a lifetime of sleepless nights. But she'd slept last night, in Reed's arms. But Reed wasn't going home with her.

"You're safe," Mr. Scott called out, but his calm assurance wouldn't be enough to settle her nerves. "One of the sheriff's deputies is watching you from the porch. I could hardly harm you with an eyewitness. And you have Annie with you…"

Barbie had had Annie with her, too. Had the little girl been an eyewitness to her nanny's murder? Sasha prayed not, and because Annie had slept so soundly the night before, Sasha figured she hadn't seen anything. Nothing that would give her the nightmares that Sasha would have to live with the rest of her life....

A life without Reed.

Unless she came back to Sunset Island.

She grasped the handle, pulling open the door to a shadowed flight of steps. She lifted Annie, carrying the toddler as she ascended to the second floor.

Mr. Scott was wiping his hands on a paint-saturated rag when they joined him in a wide-open area awash with sunshine. Tall windows looked out onto the lake where barely a wave rippled the surface.

Sasha had never seen the water so calm since she'd come to Sunset Island. An unsettling thought flitted through her head. The calm before the storm?

But whatever storm hit the island, she wouldn't be here to experience it. Once the lawyer came back over from the mainland, she would get the answers she needed and deal with the estate, then catch a ride with him back to Whiskey Bay. Because of having to wait for his return, she'd missed the ferry. But she didn't want to wait until tomorrow for another one. If she did, she might change her mind about leaving Reed.

"I'm glad you came up," Roger Scott said to Sasha, then waggled his paint-stained fingers at her niece. "Hi, Annie."

The little girl buried her face in Sasha's neck. Out of shyness or fear?

This had been a bad idea. But she hadn't dared leave the little girl with Mrs. Arnold. She didn't dare leave her with anyone, not after what had happened yesterday.

"I'm sorry we interrupted your work," she said, turning for the stairs again.

And as she did, the colors from the canvases leaning against every space of wall spun before her eyes in a kaleidoscope. They evoked the same dizzy sensation she'd experienced on the stairs the day after someone had tried to push her down them. Had Mr. Scott had anything to do with that?

"No, I was done for now. Stay," he urged. "You came to see me for a reason. What do you need?"

Nadine's killer behind bars. Her heart back from Reed. Sanity.

But she couldn't voice any of those wishes, not in front of her young niece. Instead she studied his paintings, the canvases full of much more color than anything she could see through the windows.

He'd captured the lake in every kind of mood—stormy, violent, foggy, sunny. And he'd done the house and grounds, as well, the paintings lush and vivid.

But he didn't limit himself to landscapes. He'd caught Jerry working diligently in the garden, his gnarled hands holding delicate blossoms, his craggy face soft as he admired the fruit of his labor. Mrs. Arnold on the porch, watering the hanging pots. Barbie, her youthful face alight with joy in the day, as she played with Annie.

And many, many canvases held images of Nadine. Nadine with Annie, her eyes full of love, Nadine alone and pensive, Nadine…

This was the only way Sasha would ever see her sister again. In paintings, pictures.

Only her spirit lived on…in the Scott mansion.

"You're a brilliant artist," she told him, truly awed by his talent. Then she noticed his signature, R. Scott, and she remembered seeing his work at galleries in Grand Rapids and Chicago.

"Thank you," he said, accepting the compliment as if she were one of the knowledgeable reviewers who gushed over his paintings.

"I don't know much about art," she admitted.

"But you know what you like," he said, his lips lifting in a charming smile. Charming like Charles. Nadine would have gone for him. "And that's all that matters to any artist, that someone appreciate their work."

"But you've dropped out of the art scene," she remembered aloud, then flushed over her intrusion into his personal life. "I'm sorry."

"Don't be. I stopped painting for a while. I have your sister to thank for starting me up again."

How had Nadine inspired him? Because he'd loved her, or because she'd taken all the money that should have been his and he'd had to support himself? She couldn't ask that. He wasn't a troubled teenager she could pry information out of. And she wasn't entirely sure she wanted to know.

Her arms tightened around Annie, who snuggled yet in her neck. Sasha hoped she was just sleepy.

"And she let me stay here," he said, "where the light is… perfect."

Maybe for him.

But Sasha hadn't seen much light since coming to Sunset Island. Even now the sun barely filtered through some gathering clouds. That storm was coming.

"I heard that she charged you rent," Sasha admitted.

"But never accepted the money. I should pay you. You can put it away for Annie."

Or use it to keep the house.

"I'm leaving today," she said.

He nodded, his blue eyes soft with understanding. "You're running."

She couldn't help but smile. "I thought you said people only ran away *to* Sunset Island. I'm running from…"

Running. She'd just admitted it.

"Yes, you're running."

She covered Annie's ear. "From a killer," she whispered. "I think I'm entitled."

"You're in danger?" he asked.

"Someone tried to push me down the stairs a few nights ago."

"You? The power was out. It was dark. It wasn't you who died the next day."

Barbie had. Had someone watched her leave the nursery, suspected she was Barbie and tried to kill her?

She shuddered. "I hadn't thought about that." And she wouldn't, not now. "I'm still leaving."

"I said I wanted to show you something. Over here." He pulled a canvas from the wall, tipping it toward the fading light. "This is you."

At the nursery window, the light shining on her hair and casting a shadow behind her. But it wasn't a shadow. It was a transparent reflection of herself.

Nadine.

Her breath caught, and she reached toward the canvas, wanting to touch what she could not see with her own eyes anymore. Her twin.

Annie turned her head. "Mommy," she murmured sleepily, her gaze not on Sasha but on the shadow.

"That night I saw you below the window," she remembered. "Standing in the rain." *Watching me. Watching us.*

"Yes, that night," he said, his calm voice in direct contrast to Sasha's madly beating heart.

"You saw her?" Maybe she wasn't crazy.

He nodded. "I see a lot, Sasha."

She shivered and pulled her gaze from the picture, from the image of her sister's ghost. She glanced instead through one of the long windows and glimpsed a hint of the rocky beach. "Did you see the nanny's murder?" she asked.

He glanced toward the window, too. "I see things. Not witness them."

"I don't understand."

"I see that you're running, Sasha, but not from a killer. You're running from your feelings for Reed."

Chapter Thirteen

"Do you need my help?" Dylan Matthews asked, his voice crackling through Reed's cell phone.

His laptop lay open on the desk, jammed in a corner of the spare bedroom. He tapped the keyboard as he listened to his friend.

"I've got it under control," Reed said, hoping he was right as he scrolled through the documents he'd accessed. Nadine's court records.

"Really?" Dylan asked, his doubts obvious. "You're too close. It makes it hard to see what could very well be right in front of your nose. You need a fresh set of eyes. Royce and I can be on the next ferry over."

But that would be too late. Sasha would be gone by then.

"I have another set of eyes." A beautiful blue set, but they'd proved too distracting for him to think clearly or to see the merit in her suspicion.

"Good. So you have a lead, then?"

As he perused the documents, he found it. The name that jumped out at him. The link between Nadine's past and present. And to the house…just as Sasha had suspected.

"You tell me," Reed said, not yet ready to share what he'd just found. "What have you heard about the Scott Mansion?"

"That spooky old house?" Dylan chuckled. "It's quite a legend."

Nadine's and Barbie's gruesome murders would only make it more so. If Sasha kept it and opened it as a bed and breakfast, the place would be packed all season with the morbidly curious. The thrill seekers. The lawman in him groaned while the lover in him groped for any reason for her to stay.

"Yeah," he agreed. "It's quite the legend. And it's just been brought to my attention that it's a pretty hot property, the largest private landholding left on Sunset Island. I need to know if anyone's expressed an interest in the property lately. Maybe your Fed friend can snoop around—"

"I can do you better than that. My brother-in-law—"

"That's right. The developer." Evan Quade was well known in northern Michigan as the man who'd brought prosperity to the town of Winter Falls.

"He's right here. Let me put him on."

"Sheriff Blakeslee," a deep voice said. "Dylan's told me about the trouble on Sunset Island. Whatever you need…"

"Have you heard anything about the island, specifically the Scott Mansion?"

"I heard Dylan's reply as I walked into his office."

"So just the legend stuff?" Disappointment coursed through Reed. He'd been hoping for more, for the final piece that would explain the motive for Nadine's and the nanny's murders.

"Yes, I heard that, too," he said, "as part of a sales pitch."

"What?" Maybe it was the static on the phone. "You talked to Nadine?"

"No, I had a feeling this person didn't have the owner's interest at heart. I was offered a rock-bottom price if I was willing to pay a sizable commission to the person who brought me the offer."

"Sizable?"

"A million dollars."

He sucked in a quick breath. "Just as commission for the mansion?"

"It's worth it for the price I was offered. That's a valuable piece of property—has the acreage for a golf course. The house could either be converted to a clubhouse and hotel or torn down," the developer said. He wasn't the only one who'd seen the property's potential.

Reed winced at the thought of the destruction of the house and grounds. But that was the least of his concerns. "Okay, it has potential. What I need to know is who brought you this offer."

He would need the developer's testimony. But he already knew. He'd found the name in Nadine's past.

SASHA RESPONDED to the knock at the front door, grimacing as she passed through the bloodstained foyer.

She was alone in the big house but for Annie asleep in her crib. She'd sent the sheriff's deputy down to the dock with a few boxes, so that the lawyer's boat could be quickly loaded. She'd already inconvenienced him enough.

Mrs. Arnold had gone along with the deputy to make sure the boxes got loaded. She wanted Sasha gone from Sunset Island. And the lawyer would take her away.

At the high school, she was hardly loved by every student, but she felt more welcome with the surly teenagers than she'd ever felt in this house. Behind her she heard a faint whisper. Annie's voice through the baby monitor?

"Sasha…" The whisper grew louder. Sasha wasn't surprised. If she would hear Nadine anywhere, it would be at the scene of her violent death. But she'd been quiet since yesterday afternoon, since Annie had been in danger.

The door rattled as her visitor knocked harder. Shivering against a sudden chill, Sasha opened the door to the smiling face of the lawyer. "Mr. Jorgen, I can't tell you how much I appreciate your coming back and agreeing to get me and Annie back to the mainland."

He nodded. "It's been a very emotional time for you, here in this house. I understand that you want to leave. I just want to make this easy on you, Ms. Michaelson."

The whisper softened and vibrated with fear. "Sasha…"

"Nothing about this is easy, Mr. Jorgen," she admitted with a heavy sigh. Not accepting her sister's death, not leaving the island.

"Of course. Shall we go into the dining room? I have the papers you need to sign."

She followed the big man as he hustled through the burled-oak pocket doors, his briefcase swinging at his side. "But I haven't told you what I decided."

She'd only called and asked him to come to the house and for a ride to the mainland. Away from Sunset Island. Away from the place where her twin had been murdered.

He turned back toward her, his dark eyes intense. "You can't afford the upkeep. I understand that. It bled your sister dry."

She shuddered as the image of her sister lying on the beach, throat slashed, flashed through her mind. And again she heard the whisper, calling her name, calling out in warning.

"I'm sorry," he said. "Poor choice of words."

Had it been? Or was he trying to send her a message? Like Nadine had done yesterday, like she was doing now?

"I'm sorry, too, because you don't understand," she said, trying to ignore her sister's voice. Maybe Nadine thought she was giving up the house. "I don't want to just sign off the estate."

Not when so many other people could benefit from it. Annie. Her parents. She couldn't consider that Mrs. Arnold spoke the truth, that rightful heirs had been denied the estate. "Nadine wanted me to have it."

And after reading the letter, she respected Nadine, respected her last wishes and respected her whispered warnings.

"So you want to sell it?" he asked.

"No."

He sighed, a ragged sound from his barrel chest. "You still haven't made a decision. You're wasting my time, Ms. Michaelson."

"No," she said, her patience wearing as thin as his. "That is my decision. I'm keeping it."

Something flashed behind his lenses, something hot and violent. "I'm sorry, Ms. Michaelson, but that is not an option."

"Excuse me? You read my sister's will to me just a few days ago. She gave *me* the house. There were no clauses."

"I didn't read you the entire will. Of course there were clauses. Why the hell else would I have drawn it up for Nadine?" Anger flushed his face and shook his voice. "She wanted you to have the kid. I said fine. She swore you'd be a good mother to her. And she also swore that you wouldn't want anything else from her. That you'd sign off the house. Then the estate would revert to the executor."

"The executor? But that's you."

And everything made sense. He had killed Nadine.

"Nadine was a lying bitch. She strung me along on this deal for two years when the house should have been sold, the money in our pockets. We'd already lost the buyer I had interested while I waited for the old bitch to die—"

"Mrs. Scott?" Fear pulsed in Sasha, fast and furious. She had to get away, but she was sure any sudden moves would cause a reaction from him…a decidedly violent one. She edged backward, trying to gain the door.

"Yeah, I got sick of waiting on her, just like I got sick of waiting for your sister to come to her senses. She thought she could keep me happy with some cash. She had no idea what this place is worth. She thought it made a good home for Annie." He shook his head. "But she knew she had no choice. She'd eventually have to sell. She just wanted to keep me waiting. Like you have."

"You killed Mrs. Scott?" She had to keep him talking, keep him distracted while she took another tentative step away from him.

He laughed.

"Oh, God, not Nadine. Nadine didn't kill her."

"You're sure."

No, dammit, she wasn't. And she should have been, she should have trusted her sister. But she could remember the last line she'd read of her sister's letter.

Her mistakes…

Had Mrs. Scott's murder been one of those?

"Nadine wouldn't kill anyone," she said, and she prayed she was right. And in her anger she didn't back down, didn't back away as her instincts screamed at her to do.

"No, she rescinded on her end of that deal, too. I got her the job with the old lady. Had her play up her pregnancy to get into Scott's good graces."

"And it worked," she said, nearly gagging on her praise, but feeding his ego might keep him talking. "She left the estate to Nadine."

He laughed again, the sound full of such evil that a chill raced over Sasha's skin. "You are nothing like your twin. You're so naive. No wonder you two were never close."

He was wrong. She and Nadine were close. Now. The connection that Sasha had always longed for had finally been forged between them—in death, as Nadine kept desperately calling her name. And only Sasha could hear her.

"Mrs. Scott didn't leave anything to Nadine," Jorgen explained. "She thought she was signing a petition, something about her precious damned island. Instead she was signing it away. But then the bitch held on despite her bad heart. Barbie and I struck up a deal then. And she forgot some pills here and there, so the old lady finally succumbed to the inevitable."

Sasha's breath caught at the vicious lengths to which he'd gone to claim the mansion. "Barbie was in on it."

"Not that Nadine knew," he said. "She thought the old lady died of natural causes, like everyone else. She didn't know about Barbie's involvement, but she'd forced me to use the young nurse. Nadine had changed, had gotten soft when I got her pregnant."

"You got her pregnant?" Annie couldn't be his child. She was so sweet, so innocent. And this man was pure evil.

"Part of my fee for getting her out of some legal messes. We would have made a good team if she would have stuck to the deal."

"So you killed her?"

"She gave me no choice." He turned toward her, his eyes full of vicious intent. "Just as you've given me no choice."

She turned, ready to run, when a cry rang out from upstairs, then echoed through the baby monitor lying on the hall table. "Mommy!"

He caught her arm, whirling her back.

"Annie's awake," she said. "She wants me."

"Too late. You've messed up my plan enough. This time you're going to sign those papers I brought. I'm not losing another interested buyer because of a Michaelson."

"Then you're going to kill me. You tried that night on the stairs."

"I'm glad you didn't die that night. I thought I was pushing Barbie," he admitted, "thought it was her coming out of the nursery."

Just like Mr. Scott had insinuated. Had he been part of it, too?

"She'd gotten sick of waiting, had gotten a little too pushy."

"She was in on everything," Sasha realized. "You checked with her to find out when the others would be out of the house. Then you had her take Annie for a walk." God, she was sickened by the extent of his murderous plot. She'd counseled some wild teens before, but until today, she'd never been in the presence of true evil.

"Yeah," he admitted, and the only reason he would freely admit anything was because he didn't intend to leave Sasha as a witness. "I had Barbie get the kid out of the way."

"But Annie wasn't out of the way the day you killed Barbie," she said, stalling, trying to think as the walls closed around her.

And both Nadine and Annie called out for her. She had to get away. "Annie was right there. She could have seen something."

Sweat dribbled from his top lip despite the chill in the air. "That wasn't planned. I just intended to threaten Barbie so she'd stop…"

"Blackmailing you." She drew on her years of counseling with the kids where she always tried to find the positive no matter how self-destructive their actions. "You didn't want to hurt Annie. But if you hurt me now, you'll hurt her. She'll have no one."

He shook his head. "That's not true."

Oh, God, he was going to take Annie, too.

"The sheriff will take her. I could tell he always wished she was his, resented the hell out of you for getting her instead." His dark eyes glittered with pure malice. "Maybe that's why he started sleeping with you, huh? So he could play Daddy like he did when Nadine was alive."

Like the teenagers, he was lashing out, trying to hurt her. She could handle whatever emotional pain he tried to give her. It was the physical she had to fight.

"I'll sign off the estate," she offered, her voice shaking despite her efforts to steady it, to appear calm even as terror weakened her knees. "It's yours. Just leave me alone."

"It's too late. I can't do that. You'll sign off, but then you'll leave the island. You already told the sheriff's fine deputy that you and the kid were leaving with me. Thank you for making it easy—"

"I won't go quietly. I'll fight." For her life and Annie's. The child kept crying for her, calling for her mommy.

"And if you do, the kid will die, too. Is that what you want, Sasha?"

No, she'd do anything to protect Annie. But Nadine kept whispering her warning. And Sasha knew that if she and Annie got on a boat with him, neither one of them would survive. He was that demented, demented enough to kill his own child. She couldn't risk it.

"Leave Annie here. I'll go with you."

"But the others will wonder why you're leaving her," he said, thinking of his alibi, no doubt, instead of his daughter. He'd obviously never thought of Annie or he wouldn't have killed her mother.

"We can leave, go out the back way to the dock," she said. "They should be coming up the front now." She hoped.

"Then we better get this over with. Sign the papers." His big body blocked her in by the table as he opened his briefcase, drawing papers out.

Hoping to borrow some time for the others to arrive, Sasha knocked the papers to the floor, then tried to wrench herself free of his grasp.

"You are her twin. You bitch." His fingers dug into her wrist, the one still bruised from her tumble on the stairs.

She bit her lip to hold in a cry. She wouldn't give him the satisfaction.

"You're going to sign now or I'll break your arm." He was big enough, and crazy enough, to back up his threat.

She tried to wrest free, but his fingers only tightened. And the cry slipped out, torn from her burning throat. "No! Let me go! Annie needs me."

"Nobody needs you," he said with a short, maniacal laugh, "and now you're going to die."

The door from the foyer slammed open, and Reed filled the doorway. "Let her go, Jorgen. It's over."

The lawyer reached into his briefcase, pulling a gun from an inside pocket.

"Reed!" Sasha screamed out the warning. But Reed didn't duck back out. He didn't leave her alone with the madman.

"Should have used this from the start," Albert Jorgen said, but he didn't point the gun toward the sheriff. No, he pressed the barrel to Sasha's temple. "One move, bitch, and it's all over."

"It's all over for you right now, Jorgen. Put the gun down."

The big man shook his head. "No, this and her are my ticket out of here. I have my boat parked at the dock. You're going to let me get to it, Reed, or you're going to watch your lover die. Right here, right before your eyes."

The cold barrel pressed tight to Sasha's head, she didn't dare move. Didn't breathe. She was going to die.

It didn't matter whether or not she fought. Her fate was sealed, like her sister's had been.

But Reed was here now. Reed could save her.

Instead he stepped away from the door, letting the lawyer have a clear exit out, letting the lawyer take her away. She'd known she was leaving Sunset Island today, but she hadn't thought it would be the last thing she ever did.

STEPPING ASIDE, watching Albert Jorgen drag Sasha away from him, was the hardest thing Reed had ever done. Especially when he met her eyes, wide and full of fear. And questions. How could he let her go?

It might be his only chance to save her life. And doing that was his entire focus. He heard the cries through the baby monitor, heard Annie wailing for her mommy.

"I'll bring her back, Annie. I promise," he said, as he watched Jorgen jerk her through the bloodstained foyer and onto the porch. The storm was just moving in from the lake, lightning and thunder clashing over the water.

The deputy, the one Reed had assigned to stay at the door, was coming up from the dock with Mrs. Arnold. Seeing the lawyer with the gun, the young officer drew his weapon.

"Call him off, Sheriff!" Jorgen yelled. "Or I'll kill her right here."

"You're going to kill her, anyway," Reed said, forcing his voice steady and free of the emotion tearing him apart.

"I'll let her go on the dock. Let me get to my boat, let me get out of here."

Reed had intended to get him out of the house, to get him distracted and then take him down. The lawyer was distracted now, dividing his attention between Reed and the officer on the walk.

The deputy kept his weapon, up, steady, as Reed had trained him. Mrs. Arnold cowered behind the young man, her face pale with fear.

But not as much fear as that which shone from Sasha's bright eyes. Reed glanced at her, trying to reassure her with the brief look. That was all he could afford, as his focus had to stay on Jorgen, on the finger on the trigger.

The man was shaking, his big body trembling. A boom of thunder startled him, and he flinched. He could slip and shoot Sasha.

And that was a risk that Reed couldn't take.

"You're a killer, Jorgen. I can't let you go." He knew all the details, he'd heard them while he stood in the foyer, waiting for his opportunity to intervene.

Maybe he should have waited longer, but her cry had snapped his control. He couldn't let anyone hurt her.

"Then I'm not going alone," the lawyer said, his finger contracting.

A shot rang out. And a body dropped to the boards of the porch.

Chapter Fourteen

Mrs. Arnold's scream echoed Sasha's. Reed pulled her quivering body into his arms, for her comfort and his. His arms shook as he wrapped them tightly around her. Then, over her head, he shouted at the deputy, "Radio for aero med."

But as he glanced down at the lawyer, he knew it was too late for the man. He lay dead, staring up at them, his eyes still full of evil.

"He's Annie's father," Sasha cried, her voice broken by sobs. "He's Annie's father."

"He's nobody anymore, Sasha," he reassured her. "He can't hurt you. Or Annie."

"Annie," she gasped, pulling free of his arms. She stepped over the lawyer's body, running into the house. To the child who cried for her mother.

He'd kept his promise to the little girl. And to Sasha. He'd found Nadine's killer. He stared down into the dead man's face.

Greed had driven the lawyer. He'd wanted more

when he'd already had so much…the little girl he'd never claimed until the day he'd died.

REED HAD FOUND Nadine's killer. And stopped him from killing Sasha.

More than gratitude softened Sasha's heart toward the heroic lawman. Love. She loved him.

And now, with the killer caught, she didn't have to leave the island. Unless he wanted her to….

He'd warned her up-front that after his divorce he wasn't going to love again. Maybe it was time she accepted that. But when she left Annie's room that night, hope flickered as she caught sight of the lawman leaning against her bedroom doorjamb.

"I thought you were still dealing with…"

What? Police work? The fact that he'd killed a man, for her, because she'd been so stupid she'd invited the killer inside while she was alone. Even when Nadine's whisper had warned her not to, she had put herself at risk.

"I'm sorry," she said.

"Me, too," he said, his deep voice a rumble in his chest. The chest she wanted to lay her head on as she listened to his heart beat strong and steady beneath her cheek. And she wanted that for always.

"I had to get him out of the house, Sasha. That's why I let him take you outside."

"Protecting the house?" she quipped, but she knew better. "Mrs. Arnold would have kicked your butt if you let something happen to it."

He stepped closer, his gaze intense despite her efforts at levity. "And I would have died if I'd let something happen to you."

"You kept your promise," she said, stepping into his arms. No man had ever kept his promise to her before.

Words of love burned in her throat. But she didn't dare say them. She wasn't strong enough to face his rejection if he didn't return her feelings.

Instead she chose to show him. She entwined her fingers with his and tugged him into the bedroom. And she proceeded to show him with loving sensuality exactly how she felt about him. First she rose up on tiptoe and teased his lips with little, whisper-soft kisses.

His breath shuddered out. "God, Sasha, I thought he was going to shoot you." He leaned his forehead down, pressing it against hers as he gazed deep into her eyes. "Shooting him was a risk. He might have pulled the trigger…."

And taken her with him. When she'd heard the shot, so loud, so close, she'd thought it had hit her. Even though she hadn't felt a thing, she'd thought for a moment that she was dead. Was that how it had been for Nadine? Fast? Painless? God, she hoped so.

But she hadn't died. Because she had Reed. Then. And now. Tonight she wouldn't think about the future. It was enough to know that she had one. Because of him.

"You saved me, Reed. And tonight I'm yours. Completely yours."

"Tonight," he murmured as his lips claimed hers in a tender kiss.

She ignored the little flutter of panic at his sole word choice, and instead she concentrated on the passion that burned in her blood…for Reed. Her fingers fumbled on his buttons as she hurried to undress him.

"Shhh…slow down," he said against her lips. "We have all night."

Just tonight.

She understood that now, and each kiss, each caress was bittersweet. Full of tenderness…and farewell. How many times could she say goodbye to this man?

He undressed her as he'd said. Slowly. Deliberating over each button and clasp. And just as deliberately he kissed every inch of skin he exposed.

Sasha's breath caught, trapped in her lungs as her heart beat furiously. "Reed…"

She had wanted to show him what she felt for him, wanted to show her appreciation that he had saved her life. But she was the one weak with desire. Rallying, she pressed her hands against the chest she'd frantically bared, and she pushed him back on the bed. She dragged his unzipped jeans down his legs as he laughed at her struggles.

"A little impatient, Sasha?" he teased.

"I'm tired of slow," she said. Then she climbed atop him, straddling his waist as she planted kisses along his strong jaw, the hollow below his ear, the cords straining in his neck as his breath shuddered out. His hands shook as he caught her head, bringing her mouth back to his for desperate kisses.

His fingers unclasped her bra and pulled it from her

shoulders, then he lifted her higher, pulling the tip of one breast into his mouth. Tormenting the swollen nipple with the tip of his tongue and the sharp edge of his teeth.

She moaned his name, his sweet torture bringing her to the brink of ecstasy. Then he reached between them, between her legs, teasing her more, sending her over the edge.

"Reed!" And then he was inside her, driving her up again and again until she sobbed his name. As he joined her, a ragged cry slipped through his lips.

Her name.

Just her name.

She waited, but no declaration of love followed. And she began to accept that it never would.

WATCHING HER SLEEP, curled up in his arms, was the fulfillment of every fantasy he'd ever had. Reed wanted this opportunity every night. It didn't matter how short a time he'd known her, or how badly he'd been hurt before, he loved her. And because he loved her, he had to let her go.

She moaned and brushed her lips against his chest, her eyes opening. "Ummm…good morning."

Was it? What he had to do was nearly as difficult as watching Jorgen hold that gun to her head the day before.

"Why so serious?" she asked, running a fingertip along his lower lip.

He resisted the urge to kiss it, to kiss her luscious

mouth, swollen from their passion the night before. God, he loved her. Loved everything about her.

"It's all over now," she said.

After what he had to tell her, it might be. She hadn't left yesterday, but she'd be leaving today.

"Not all of it, Sasha."

She sighed. "I know you took it easy on me yesterday." She moved against him. "Maybe not last night. But yesterday you spared me. You'll need my statement."

"I heard pretty much everything he told you, Sasha. I know about the house."

"That it wasn't Nadine's."

An ache pounded at his temple. He squeezed his eyes against the pain and the light filtering through her blinds. "And it's not yours."

She drew in a quick breath. "I know that. Morally I know I have to give it back. But…"

"But what?" Maybe he'd misread her. Maybe she was more like his ex…and Nadine…than he'd thought. He shouldn't have trusted his heart.

Her face flushed. "I can't explain. But I feel close to my sister here. Closer than we ever were when she was alive. I don't want to lose that."

"You have to let her go, Sasha." His heart contracted as he felt her pain, her loss. He couldn't take that away, but maybe he could help her deal with it. "She's dead. Her killer is dead now."

She jerked free of his arms and slipped out from under the blankets. "I knew you wouldn't understand."

"Tell me."

"Why? You want me out of here? How long do Annie and I have to clear out, Sheriff?" Bitterness twisted those swollen lips, and anger swirled in the blue depths of her eyes.

"Sasha…"

"What? It isn't like that? It is like that, Reed. You want me out of here. You want me gone." And along with the anger, he heard her pain. She thought it was personal.

"The house wasn't Nadine's to give. It belongs to Mrs. Scott's rightful heirs."

"I wasn't talking about just the house. You want me off the island. Since the killer is dead, you don't have to protect me. Now you're protecting yourself."

She knew him better than he'd thought. Better than maybe he knew himself. He couldn't deny her accusations. And he couldn't fight them. He loved her, but she wouldn't stay. It would hurt when she left today, but it would hurt a lot more when she left later…after he'd gotten used to waking up with her in his arms.

"You're being unreasonable," he said, throwing back the covers. "You know this is the right thing to do…."

"For who, Reed? You think this is the right thing for you?" she asked, her voice full of disbelief. "For Annie? For me? I know you were hurt once, badly. So was I."

"So you know it would be crazy for us to let this go any further. We'd only get hurt." But his aching heart told him it was already too late.

THINGS HAD ALREADY GONE too far. She loved him. Should she have told him? But then he might have stayed to help her finish packing. And since she'd done most of that the day before, it wouldn't have taken her long. Then he might have escorted her right off the island.

Sasha understood protecting one's heart. She'd tried that for a long time.

But she'd never loved anyone like this. There was no protection against emotions this powerful. But Reed didn't feel the same way, hadn't let himself feel the same.

He could let her go.

And so she had to. Or she could throw herself at him, beg for his love. She'd suffered humiliation for love before, for a man who hadn't been worth it. Reed was worth it.

She shook her head. He was too strong. Tears, pleas, none of that would sway him, would make him ask her to stay. Only love would do that.

"You don't have to leave," said a deep voice, interrupting her thoughts.

Not Reed's.

And not Charles. She'd talked to him already, not letting him past the front door this time. He'd wanted her to return to the mainland with him. She'd sent him off alone with no doubt in his mind that she would ever play substitute for Nadine again. Before turning toward the door, Sasha glanced back over her shoulder, to where the empty rocker gently moved back and forth.

Then she greeted the man who stood in the nursery

doorway. Mr. Scott. "I appreciate that." Especially after the scheme her sister had helped run on his poor mother.

"I mean it," he said. "I'll continue staying in the carriage house. This house is too big and too full of memories for me."

"But what about your…"

He grimaced. "My daughters? Mrs. Arnold will never learn to keep her mouth shut. My daughters don't visit me, Ms. Michaelson."

"I'm sorry…" She couldn't imagine not having a close relationship with her parents the way Nadine hadn't. That was a regret Nadine would never be able to make up. Nor would her parents.

"I am, too," he admitted. "It's my fault. I was never a father to them."

"So give them the house. Mrs. Arnold said that's what your mother would have wanted."

"But it's not what they want. They have their own lives," he said with a regretful sigh, probably because they didn't include him. "People don't come to Sunset Island to live. Remember what I told you. They come here to hide, to run away from their problems."

"Like Nadine." She'd been hiding from all her mistakes. The lawyer had taken advantage of that, of her.

"And the sheriff," Mr. Scott pointed out.

She knew Reed was hiding, from his pain, his past and now from her. "It's a beautiful place. I could see someone building a life here, staying because they wanted to, not because they have no other choice."

And she'd stay…if Reed asked her.

"You remind me of my oldest daughter," he said. "She's a social worker."

"I'm a school counselor."

"The jobs are close. So are the attitudes. You're caring women, strong women."

Yeah, she was strong. She'd be okay. But she'd be alone except for Annie. She thanked God and Nadine for the little girl. But Annie needed more than just her. Annie needed Reed. Too.

With the house, she had a connection to Nadine. But that wasn't fair. Not to Mr. Scott. Not to her. She couldn't wait around, hoping that Reed would love her.

She had to leave. That was what he wanted.

So he could keep hiding.

"I really have no choice." Not legally. Not emotionally. "I have to go."

"I figured you for stubborn. So I brought you something." He stepped into the hall, bringing a canvas back with him. The painting of her standing in the nursery window and Nadine standing just behind her.

"I can't accept this…"

But like the house, she wanted it, wanted another connection to her sister, wanted proof that she hadn't lost her mind when she'd heard her sister's ghost. But she knew what one of his paintings was worth, and it was too much.

"Nonsense." He waved away her concern. "It's yours. You're the only one who would truly appreciate it."

And because he was right, she had to take it. And again she thought, what a strange man. "Thank you."

He nodded. "Goodbye, then, Ms. Michaelson. It was nice meeting you."

And he left her, to go back to the carriage house, back into hiding. From himself. From the mistakes he'd made.

Was she making one by leaving without a fight?

HE WATCHED HER BOARD the ferry, Annie in her arms. The wind came in off the lake, teasing her long black locks, tangling them around her face. God, she was beautiful. The most beautiful woman he'd ever seen.

And he was letting her go.

He had to let her go now.

It would only hurt more later. But as his heart contracted, he had to admit it hurt damned bad now.

"Sasha!" Her name tore free of his throat, unbidden.

She turned toward him, her gaze meeting his. But she didn't say anything.

He moved toward the gangplank. "I have something for you," he said, taking Nadine's letter from his pocket. "I don't need it anymore."

Jorgen's admission was enough evidence. He didn't need anything else.

No, that was a lie. He needed Sasha. And Annie.

The little girl reached toward him. "Wed…"

Her little face was pinched with anxiety. She had never ridden the ferry before. For trips to the mainland, Reed had taken her in the sheriff's boat.

"She doesn't want to go," he said. And he didn't want to let either of them go.

Sasha nodded. "Neither do I."

His heart beat faster, as hope rose. "Then why are you leaving?"

"Because it's what you want." Tears dampened her eyes…like a sucker punch to Reed's gut.

God, it was the last thing he wanted. "Sasha…that's not true."

"What's true then, Reed?"

He released a ragged sigh, but his lungs still burned with breath held too long. "That you'll leave eventually. You won't stay here. There's no high school here. Really no entertainment. You'd be bored."

Her eyes glowed as she stared at him. He refused to accept that it was love, because that made him an even bigger fool for letting her leave.

"I'd never be bored," she said, her eyes shining even brighter as her gaze locked with his. "But you're right. I'd leave."

He sucked in a quick, painful breath. Having his fear confirmed didn't make it hurt any less.

"I'd leave every day," she continued. "Like you ordinarily do."

But these hadn't been ordinary times for him…not since Nadine's murder and Sasha's arrival.

"I'd go to the mainland," she said. "To one of the high schools there. Or maybe I wouldn't go every day. With the size of the schools, maybe they would only need me a couple days a week. And every night I'd come back here. To you. And Annie."

He sucked in another breath, this one full of excitement and hope. Could he believe her? Could he let himself trust another woman's promises?

When that woman was Sasha, he could. "Come down here. I have something to give you."

"The letter. I know," she said, uttering a soft sigh. "I don't need it. I thought I needed the house, the letter, something to connect me to Nadine. But here—" She jiggled the child in her arms, getting a laugh out of her. "I have everything I need."

"Everything you need?"

Despite her words, she walked back down the gangplank, back to the dock, back to him. "No, not everything," she admitted.

"What else do you need, Sasha?"

"You, Reed. I need you."

"Why?" he asked as his heart leaped, lighter than it had been since he'd met her and he'd thought he'd have to let her go.

"Because I love you. I know it hasn't been very long or the best of circumstances, but I love you."

"I don't have much to offer you, Sasha," he felt inclined to point out. Material things had always mattered so much to his ex-wife. "The cottage is pretty primitive."

"I don't care where I live. True, I didn't want to leave the mansion, but it wasn't because of its size."

"It was because of Nadine, your connection to her

there." He understood that, and it had killed him to tell her she had to leave it.

She nodded, tears gleaming again in her eyes. "But I'd rather have you whisper my name in the night."

"What?"

"I'm a little nuts," she said with a short laugh. "Can you deal with that?"

"The only thing I can't deal with is losing you. But is this fair to you, Sasha? This isn't the life you left behind in Grand Rapids."

"No, it's not. That life was empty," she said. "This life will be full…with you, with Annie."

"I can't give you much, not on the salary of a small-town sheriff."

"I've never had much. I won't miss it."

And he believed that. He trusted her. And so he laid it all out, his heart.

"I can give you a home, as simple as it is—"

"I always liked your cottage more than the mansion." Her soft voice rang with sincerity.

"And I can give you a father for Annie." Neither of them would mention again the man who had been her father.

"And I can give you a man who will love you and only you for the rest of your life."

He thought of her comments about Nadine, about what she'd heard, what she'd believed. "And beyond," he added.

She smiled as he folded both her and Annie into his arms. "I love you, oh, how I love you, Reed Blakeslee. And I'll love you…forever."

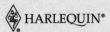

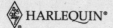

If you enjoyed what you just read,
then we've got an offer you can't resist!

Take 2 bestselling
love stories FREE!

Plus get a FREE surprise gift!

Silhouette® BOMBSHELL™

BRINGS YOU THE THIRD
POWERFUL NOVEL IN

LINDSAY McKENNA's

SERIES

Sisters of the Ark:

Driven by a dream of legendary powers,
these Native American women have
sworn to protect all that their people
hold dear.

WILD WOMAN

by *USA TODAY* bestselling author
Lindsay McKenna

Available April 2005
Silhouette Bombshell #37

Available at your favorite retail outlet.

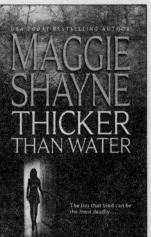

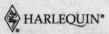